T0208409

Broomstick Tales
Time for This Witch To Come Home

Told by Wazoo the Wizard
Written and illustrated by
Arnie Grimm

authorHOUSE®

AuthorHouse™
1663 Liberty Drive
Bloomington, IN 47403
www.authorhouse.com
Phone: 833-262-8899

Published by AuthorHouse 10/05/2020

ISBN: 978-1-7283-4964-0 (sc)
ISBN: 978-1-7283-4962-6 (hc)
ISBN: 978-1-7283-4963-3 (e)

Library of Congress Control Number: 2020919068

Print information available on the last page.

To all my readers…
Whom I have given copies to,
Whom I have met and bought my books,
Whom I haven't met and bought my books,
Thank you.
To my friends and relatives who know me and still bought my books, thank you.
And finally to my wife Karen thank you for forty five years of happily ever after.

Contents

Chapter One
Timing is Everything

Astronomers claim anywhere you look in space there isn't a center of the universe. When it comes to magic though, there is a center of the magical world. It is in the town of Broomstick, at the Hidden Quiddity Potion Shop.

If you haven't visited the potion shop lately, I suggest you take time out of your busy day and drop in. As you know, this potion shop carries everything you would ever need to do magic. It may not always be what you want, but trust me you'll find exactly what you need.

On the shelves stood bottles filled with the most common ingredients used in making potions, elixirs, charms, and spells.

You might catch a special on dried soapwort root or entangled creeping thyme for your potionized herb garden.

Pay special attention to the Red Dragon tail skin jar. "Just a small smidgen in a potion will sizzle up the magic," exclaimed Harriet while making up her love potions.

"Sizzzzzzzzzzzzz."

You would not find any Voodoo or Black magic stuff as it was forbidden by Magical Law.

Behind the counter were drawers labeled 'Magic Wands'. There were beginner wands that are filled with slug drool to keep magic from happening too fast. Magic wands for adolescents came filled with spider web silk for smooth action of magic. The type of web silk depended on the type of spider you teenager was attracted to. Of course black widow web filled wands were forbidden for anyone under a half century old.

Over in one corner were broomsticks, flying broomsticks. The broomstick would be enchanted with all the up to date features. On a side wall were the shelves that contained various sizes of cauldrons, pouches, and leather covered journals with parchment paper pages. Up on the top shelf sat an object of interest to all that came into the potion shop. One tarnished oil lamp with a sign that hung on it 'NOT FOR SALE'.

The Hidden Quiddity Potion Shop was owned by two sisters, Agnes and Harriet. Whatever happens in the magical world, it is assured to come to Agnes and Harriet's attention. Do I need to tell you? Agnes and Harriet are witches.

Oh who am I you ask? I'm your story teller, I am Wazoo the Wizard and this Broomstick Tale is called Time for this Witch to Come Home.

I would like to say our story has started on time, but I can't. The story is on time, that is to say it is about time. What I meant to say is this is a timeless tale of time. You will understand in time. Oh it's time to just start telling you the story.

The Keystone family had decided that they had enough of the big city turmoil of day in and day out living in traffic and close quarters. It was time for a change. Howard and Melissa Keystone started to look for a small town to move to. Every night at the dinner table one or the other would have found a name of a small town that day.

"What about Crestwood? Its population is seventeen thousand two hundred and five," said Howard.

"No, still too big," said Melissa.

"What about us? Don't we get any say in this?" asked their oldest son, Fitzpatrick. "I need a good college to attend."

"Only when your mother is satisfied with the choice," said Howard.

The Keystone's had three children, two boys and one girl. The oldest at nineteen is Fitzpatrick, then seventeen year old Donavan, and lastly at the early preteen age of twelve is Natalie.

These evening conversations went on for months until one night at dinner Howard said, "I found this ad in this unusual newsmagazine that was delivered to our office. It was kind of funny that no one wanted to pick it up. They all acted like it had a hex on it."

Howard showed Melissa the front cover. She read the title aloud, "Once in a Lifetime Job Opportunity." Melissa sat there with a grimace expression.

When Howard read the description, it was as if someone else was speaking. "A small bakery in a small quiet town, with plenty of good customers, and an excellent money return. This business also comes with a ranch style home on thirteen acres with friendly neighbors."

While reading this Melissa and the others observed the front cover. There was a shadowed face that seemed to be talking. It made the hair on the back of Melissa's neck stand up on end.

"It is in the town of Broomstick. We can just go look. We can make it our vacation destination this year." said Howard.

Melissa sat back away from the dinner table and said, "When things seem to be too good to be true, they aren't true at all."

A few days had gone by when Melissa happened to pick up the newsmagazine. She thumbed through it looking at the articles reading the headlines. "Humans marrying others from space. Pyramids discovered buried under Mars surface by digging rover. Cats talk to humans through brain waves."

Melissa turned the page and saw a public service announcement. "Warning: Raising children in the big city is like living in a haunted castle with the un-dead feasting on your souls at night." A chill came over her like being in a cemetery on a cold December night. She quickly turned the page and read on.

There were all kinds of ads for strange jobs, jobs in strange places, and strange jobs in strange places. Each had earnings of over a million dollars for one day of work. Then she read the full page ad that Howard was looking at. It wasn't one of the get rich quick scheme.

Melissa read aloud to herself, "A small bakery in the friendly town of Broomstick is waiting for you and your family. A ranch house with land included."

She glanced through the small print of the details. "Someone must have passed away and left it to someone that doesn't want it," thought Melissa.

That evening at dinner Melissa said to Howard, "Let's check out your strange little town of Broomstick."

"You mean it? You really want to go to see this one?" asked Howard.

"Where is Broomstick?" asked Fitzpatrick.

"What a screwy name for a town," said Donavan.

"I like the name. It has a pleasant sound to it," said Natalie.

Donavan poked Natalie with his fork under the table.

"Donavan jabbed me with his fork," said Natalie.

"No I didn't, she's lying again," said Donavan.

Natalie knew it wouldn't do any good to complain. Her parents had never believed her when she told them that her older brothers were abusing her.

"Go to your room Natalie," said Howard.

Natalie grabbed one more bite of food and stomped away from the dinner table to her room. Mukul was waiting for Natalie in her room. "What was it this time?" Mukul asked.

"A Jab with a fork," said Natalie as she flopped on the bed.

"So what is with this big idea to visit Broomstick?" asked Mukul.

"Some place that dad found in this strange magazine. It has a bakery and a house for sale," explained Natalie.

"I've been to Broomstick. It's a very nice place to live. I have friends there I could introduce you to," said Mukul.

Natalie's bedroom door opened and her mother came in. "I heard you talking to your stuffed toy again. What have I told you about that?"

"I'm sorry mom. I will stop talking to my toys," said Natalie.

"Is your homework done for tomorrow?" asked Melissa.

"Yes mom and Mukul…" Natalie stopped quickly and restarted her words. "…and I rechecked all my work for errors."

Melissa stood there for a moment looking at the stuff toy. It was a worn handmade black cat that was given to Natalie many years ago from her great, great, grandmother Shasta not too long before she passed away. Melissa remembered what she had made Natalie promise.

Great, great, grandmother Shasta said to Natalie, "Keep Mukul close to you at all times. Never allow anyone to take him away from you. He will protect you."

"Don't you think it is time to get rid of that stuffed toy, Natalie?" asked Melissa.

Natalie looked at her mom then at Mukul. "How about if I got a box and some tissue paper and wrapped it up carefully and put it away for when I have children," said Natalie. "That way I will keep great, great, grandma's promise and you will be happy that I won't be talking to it."

7

Melissa said, "Alright, I'll get you a box tomorrow and we will put it up in the attic."

Natalie faked a smile knowing very well that this was her mom's opportunity to get a hold of that raggedy old toy and dispose of it for good.

"Brush your teeth and don't forget to floss then go right to bed," said Melissa.

"Yes mom," was all Natalie said.

After her mom left, Natalie whispered to Mukul "What are we going to do? You know she will throw you away!"

"Not to worry my little protégée. I have a plan. I think it is time to tell you who I am," said Mukul.

Chapter Two
Mukul the Black Cat

Natalie saw Mukul as a real black cat that could talk. At times he stood up on two legs and walked like a human while other times he acted like a cat. Others saw him as a stuffed old handmade raggedy toy cat.

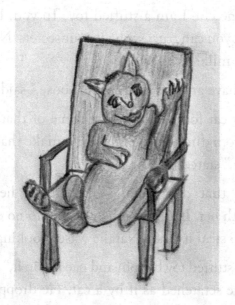

Mukul surprised Natalie one day not long after she had received him from her great, great grandmother. She was only seven years old at the time. They were alone in her bedroom when Mukul spoke up.

"Excuse me. Can you get me a glass of milk and some food," said Mukul.

Natalie turned to where she had laid the handmade stuffed toy cat. There in its place sat a cat. Not like a cat should sit. He was sitting in a doll's chair like a human would sit with his legs crossed.

"Are…, are you talking to me?" asked Natalie.

"There is no one else in the room little one, so yes I am talking to you," said Mukul.

"Who are you?" asked Natalie.

"I'm your stuffed handmade raggedy black cat that your great, great grandmother gave you. My name is Mukul."

"Mom will be upset. I can't have any pets," said Natalie.

"To everyone else I am a stuffed toy. To you, I am your one true friend that you can trust with all your secrets. Now how about some food and milk?" said Mukul.

"We don't have any cat food in the house," said Natalie.

"I don't eat cat food. How about some of that fried chicken and coleslaw from dinner last night? And make that iced tea with a lemon wedge," stated Mukul.

Ever since that day Natalie has carried her stuffed toy everywhere with her. It annoyed her mother to no end. Her older brother tried to steal it when Natalie wasn't looking.

"Owe, that stuffed toy has pin and needles in it," said Donavan. His hands were scratched as if by a cat. He dropped the toy on the floor.

Natalie picked up Mukul and said, "That's what you get when you try to steal my cat."

Natalie was now twelve and her mother wanted to get rid of that stuffed toy. She had caught Natalie talking to it on many occasions over the years. She could only hear Natalie's side of the conversation.

Her brothers would tattle on her and would do terrible things to her. Fitzpatrick put white glue in her toothpaste tube. He left out a piece of gum for her to find. It was onion gum from a prank store.

Donavan was the worst. He put an exploding popper under the toilet seat. When Natalie would sit down, a loud bang would scare her. When no one was watching he would hit her, poke her, or pull her hair.

Natalie's parents wouldn't believe her and even accused her of making up stories and outright lying. She spent a lot of time in her room with Mukul the cat.

Now it came down to putting the stuffed cat in a box and giving it to her mom to put up in the attic. Natalie knew what her mother was really going to do with the stuff cat. She was going to throw it away forever.

Mukul picked this time to tell Natalie who he was. "I was your great, great grandmother's, ah, familiar. She was the last witch in your family. Strangely the magic didn't pass to others in your family. When you were born, your great, great grandmother felt the magic was in you. She knew something that no one ever expected to happen. You inherited the family's magical powers," said Mukul.

"I heard mom refer to great, great grandmother as that old witch. She meant it to be awful. I hated it when she called her that," said Natalie. "Am I a witch?"

"Not yet," said Mukul. "Your magical powers are not activated yet. They are dormant inside you. I also hold the key to your future."

"The key to my future, what is it? What does it look like? Can I see it?" asked Natalie.

"It's your great, great grandmother's magical amulet. When it is the right time I will give it to you and all your beautiful magical abilities will come to life," exclaimed Mukul with brightened eyes. "For now I have to plan for tomorrow. Sleep now for tomorrow will bring a new awareness."

While Natalie slept, Mukul got very busy. First, he found a needle and thread. Then, some leftover scraps of material. He sat there in the den watching late night television while he sewed a pocket pouch with a drawstring that could hang around Natalie's neck.

Mukul also stopped off at the refrigerator for his usual midnight snack of leftovers from dinner. He helped himself to a drink of milk straight out of the carton while nibbling at the leftover ham that was to be used for sandwiches the next day.

Later that night he walked around the house visiting each room. He took something from each family member. Mukul collected bits of finger nails, hair from various places of the body, flaked off dried skin, and dried blood. He was very meticulous in gathering these remnants. The pocket pouch was nearly full by morning. The last item to go in the pouch was a Botswana Eye agate.

When Natalie got up the next morning, Mukul was sitting in his chair waiting for her. "Before you go off to school we need to take care of some business. Take my paw with your left hand and extend out your right hand palm down."

Natalie got down on her knees and faced Mukul. She grabbed hold of his paw and held out her right hand palm down. "Like this?" Natalie asked.

"Now repeat after me each word. Do not stop or ask questions. You will feel a slight electrical shock run through you. Keep a hold of my paw," said Mukul. "Are you ready?"

Natalie was excited. She guessed this was going to be something done with magic. "Yes I'm ready."

Mukul began to recite the spell. "Stephen sevphen ou yu do yu."

Natalie repeated, "Stephen sevphen ou yu do yu."

"Quarter, half, end of a staff," continued Mukul.

"Quarter, half, end of a staff," repeated Natalie.

"Imitator, simulator, impersonator, faker. I am a copycat maker," said Mukul.

"Imitator, simulator, impersonator, faker. I am a copycat maker," said Natalie.

A surge of energy spun through Natalie's mind as she held on to Mukul's paw. Never in her life has she ever felt what was going through her. It was like an electrical shock from a nine volt battery on one's tongue with ice cold water from a water fall drenching you.

After it was all over Natalie opened her eyes. Under her right hand was a handmade raggedy toy cat. "Oh Mukul, please don't leave me." She picked up the stuffed toy and began to cry.

"Incredible. It even fooled you," said Mukul standing off in a corner.

Natalie turned around to look at the voice. "What did we do?"

"We made a copy of my appearance that everyone else sees. But you have to be very careful not to let anyone see the real me," said Mukul. "When you come home from school put that one in the box."

Natalie laid the copycat down on the floor next to her toy box and went to school.

When Natalie walked in the door from school, her mother was waiting right there with a shoebox. Natalie took the shoebox and walked into her room. Her mother was right behind her.

Natalie carefully wrapped the stuffed toy cat and put it in the box. She placed the lid on top and handed it to her mother. "We can also put my toy box up there, I won't need my toys anymore," said Natalie with a different attitude toward life.

Melissa tilted her head and peered at Natalie quizzically as she took the shoebox. She didn't say anything. She just turned and walked out of Natalie's bedroom.

Mukul came out from under the bed and sat down in the doll chair. "I have something for you that will keep you safe. No one will ever hurt you again."

He handed the pouch to Natalie. "Wear this around your neck and never take it off. Don't count on it to protect you. Heed this warning. Don't use it to do any harm. It will do what it needs to do to protect you. Do you understand?"

Natalie nodded as she pulled it over her head and down onto her neck.

"Now go get the phone book and bring it back here," said Mukul.

Natalie went into the kitchen to get the phone book. Donavan was in there making a ham sandwich and filling a glass with milk. He picked up the mustard bottle and pointed it at Natalie's back. But when he squeezed it the plastic bottle broke at the bottom end and splattered Donavan with mustard.

At the same time their mother came into the kitchen and witnessed the doomed prank. "Mom, Natalie squirted me with mustard," said Donavan.

Melissa stood right in front of her son. "I saw what you tried to do. Go and get cleaned up then come back here to clean up the mess you made in the kitchen. Also you are grounded for a week."

Natalie was shocked at what just took place. She didn't get blamed for what Donavan did. With the phone book in her hands she backed out of the kitchen and made a bee line back to her bedroom.

"What are you in trouble for this time," asked Mukul.

"Nothing, Mom caught Donavan trying to squirt me with mustard and grounded him for a week," said Natalie.

She put the phone book on her desk and sat down. "What am I looking for in the phone book, a witchcraft store?"

"Something like that. Look under metaphysical," said Mukul.

Natalie thumbed through the pages, "Meat wholesale. Medical supplies. Men's clothing. Metal machinery. Metaphysical. Wow it's really in here."

She read aloud, "Psychic Journey Herbal Store. Master's Eye Books and Potions. Ancient Ways Magikal Supplies."

"Find the closest one you can walk to," requested Mukul.

"Here's one, Celestial Encounters, all your needs for herbs, books, candles and more," read Natalie.

"That will do for what we need. Write this down," said Mukul.

Natalie pulled out her note book from school and took out a pen and notebook paper. Mukul jumped up onto the desk.

"You will need a handmade leather bound journal, a bottle of ink, and a quill. Look to see if they have a small fist sized cauldron. If they do, get a pouch of dragon's blood incense. Pick out two candlestick holders, two dark red bee's wax candles, and a box of wood matches."

"What is all this for? Oh, are we going to do dark black magic spells by candlelight?" asked Natalie.

"No! And don't ever say black magic again. I will warn you now, black magic is dangerous and leads to an early death or worse," said Mukul. "No one can control black magic. It controls you and destroys all that you love."

Natalie had never seen Mukul so upset before. "I... I'm sorry. I was only joking."

Seeing Mukul like that scared Natalie to the bone.

"I know that, but the powers that surround us don't know that," warned Mukul. "Tell your mother that you are going to the craft store to buy supplies for a school project and that you need money."

"I can't lie to my mother. It didn't matter whether she believed me or not I made sure I always told her the truth for my own sake," said Natalie.

"You will not be lying. You are going to a craft store, a witchcraft store. And starting tonight you will be enrolled in a very privileged witchcraft school," said Mukul.

Natalie got up and went to her mother that was in the den folding clothes. "Mom I need some money to buy craft supplies for a school project. I can walk to the craft store. It is not far."

"A school project? Now this sounds better than playing with that old stuffed toy," said Melissa. She gave Natalie some money and smiled.

Natalie scurried out the door. She was energized with excitement of what this strange stuff was for. Suddenly Donavan jumped out of the bushes in front of Natalie. "You got me grounded you little snot, and that is going to cost you the money that mom just gave you."

"I didn't do anything. You caused your own bad luck," said Natalie.

Donavan moved to grab Natalie. But when he touched her with his fingers, fire engulfed them until he pulled his hand away. He was in horrific pain with blistered fingertips.

Natalie just walked away leaving her brother screaming and crying.

Chapter Three
The Metaphysical Store

Natalie stared at the storefront window display. There were books on many different kinds of magic, various shaped bottles, and unusual gadgets that she had no idea what they were for.

The incense filled the air just outside the door as if it were inviting her to come in. To a twelve year old girl this was the most taboo and eerie experience that could ever happen to her.

Behind the counter was a dark haired and dark skinned woman with black pearl eyes. "Ah, you come seeking enlightenment. My reading room awaits, twenty dollars."

Natalie slowly pulled out the list written on notebook paper. "I need a handmade leather bound journal with a bottle of ink and a quill."

"Over there in the corner," said the woman.

Natalie looked over at where she pointed, then turned back and continued to read the list. "I also need a small fist size cauldron and a pouch of dragon's blood incense, two candlestick holders and dark red bee's wax candles."

The woman peered at Natalie with suspicion. "Cauldrons are over there with the incense and the candles and holders are in the back corner."

Natalie inspected the cauldrons thoroughly from the large melon size down to the size of an orange. She picked out a small cauldron and a pouch of dragon blood incense.

Over in the first corner was the leather bound journals. Natalie set down the cauldron and incense to pick up one of the leather books. She ran her hand over the cover. It was stamped with mysterious symbols. None of them meant anything to her. Instead, she picked one with an iris flower on the front. The ink bottles and quills were plain and came in a box.

Natalie sat her items on the counter and went back to the corner where the candlestick holders were. Some were with strange mythical creatures and others were just outright scary. Then she saw the pair of dragons that were posed around pillars as if they were guarding a secret entrance. They were too high for her to reach. "I would like the pair of dragon candlestick holders please."

The woman came over with a step stool and climbed up to the upper shelf. She handed them one at a time down to Natalie.

Natalie set them down carefully on the counter and stood there admiring them. The woman brought over two dark red bee's wax candles.

The woman gazed at Natalie with her black pearl eyes. "Are you sure about what you are buying? It seems like you might be doing something you're not old enough to be getting into. You're not doing voodoo?"

"Oh my no, I am getting school supplies to go to witchcraft school," said Natalie.

The woman looked at Natalie and cocked her head sideways. "Witchcraft school? Girl, someone is pulling your leg. There is no such thing as witchcraft school. And between you and me and the wall all this stuff is nonsense. I just sell it because of people like you that want to believe in magic can have their fun. You go and have your fun at witchcraft school," laughed the woman.

She was still laughing when Natalie walked out of the shop. "Humph, I don't think she believes in magic at all."

Natalie walked into the house and saw Donavan in the kitchen with his hand in a bowl of ice water. She made a bee line to her room to hide her purchases. Natalie sat down the paper bag and slid it under her bed.

"What have you done?" said Natalie to Mukul. "My brother's fingers were burned after he touched me."

"He wasn't just going to touch you. He was going to do you physical harm. I told you that pouch will protect you. But remember, if you provoke him it will not help you," said Mukul.

At the dinner table the mood was other than congenial. For the first time Natalie sat on the one side of the table by herself. Donavan was attempting to eat with his left hand. His other hand was bandaged up. Nothing had been said about what happened to Donavan's hand.

Their father was doing most of the talking. "I got my vacation scheduled for the whole month of July. I understand in Broomstick they have a renaissance faire going on that month."

"Did you contact the seller of the bakery? I don't want to go there and have it already sold," said Melissa.

Howard smiled with a wide grin. "I did better than that. I already agreed to buy it. We'll own it free and clear in ten years. I couldn't resist when the guy on the phone told me what he wanted for the bakery and the property."

"Tell me you didn't just send someone down payment money without knowing who they are?" asked Melissa.

"Oh, no of course not, the actual transaction will happen when we go there in July. We will get a chance to back out of the deal. Winston Wisestone assured me this is a legitimate offer."

"I'll start tomorrow looking for a place to stay that will be affordable for the entire month," said Melissa.

"Not necessary, we are going to stay at the ranch house for free," said Howard.

"I'm beginning to get that uneasy feeling this has a catch to it that we can't afford," said Melissa.

It was Natalie's turn to help in the kitchen after dinner. She was alone with her mother who was putting away the leftover food while she loaded the dishwasher. "Mom, are we moving to Broomstick?" asked Natalie.

"No, we're just going to visit and take a look. I don't think this bakery business is on the level," said Melissa. "Did you get what you needed for your school project?"

"I think so. I haven't started it just yet. Did Donavan say what happened to his fingers?" inquired Natalie.

"Your brother is in real big trouble. I caught him in the garage out of his room. I think he burned his fingers doing something stupid with gasoline. Lucky for us he didn't burn the whole house down," said Melissa.

"It's Friday, can I stay up a little late and work on my project. I promise I'll be quiet," asked Natalie.

"Yes of course you may. You see maturing isn't so hard or painful. Just giving up a security blanket was your first step." Natalie's mom took a step toward her to give her a hug. Natalie was horrified as to what was going to happen.

Melissa gave her a hug and said, "Tomorrow I want to see what your school project is. Maybe I can help."

Natalie hurried up and finished cleaning the kitchen and got back to her room quickly. "Whew, that was a close one."

"What was a close one?" asked Mukul.

"Mom gave me a hug. I was worried that she was going to burst into flames," said Natalie.

Mukul stood there and laughed. Then he got very serious. "We both have things to do tonight."

"So are we going to play witchcraft school?" asked Natalie.

This was the second time Natalie saw Mukul get angry. "Maybe you are not ready. The timing might not be right for this to happen. But it is too late for me to stop what is already in motion. I'm not playing any games. Magic carries great responsibility. A witch must be faithful to her place in nature. Eventually you will learn the promise of the witch: 'I am the guardian of all that is right'. Do you still think this is a game?"

"Na...no, I think you are very serious. I might need a little more time to think about this though," said Natalie.

"Don't think too long, you must decide tonight. Listen very closely and do what I tell you. Prior to midnight set up your desk with the candlestick holders on each side. In between the candlesticks place the cauldron with a pebble size of the dragon's blood incense inside," instructed Mukul. "Place the leather journal with the ink bottle and quill on the desk."

Natalie pulled out the paper bag from under her bed and sat it up on her desk for later as Mukul continued to talk.

"Follow these instructions exactly without making a mistake. Listen for the clock tower to toll the first bell of midnight. Strike a single wood match and light the left candlestick. Wait for the sixth bell before you light a second match. Light the incense and let it fill the room. When the eleventh bell tolls light a third match, and hold it to the wick of the right candlestick. Then sit facing forward with your hands palms down on the top of the desk. Sit quietly and wait for the twelfth toll."

Natalie started to say something, but Mukul waved a paw at her. "I must leave for a while, don't forget my instructions." Like a spinning top Mukul vanished into thin air.

Natalie was alone with her thoughts for the first time in her life. She felt cold, helpless, and unloved. Her excitement in learning magic and becoming a witch had just turned into a scary nightmare of gray gloom of despair.

Natalie set up her desk just as Mukul had said to, then she stood back to look at it. It had a look of foreboding. The two dragons stared at her with hard red eyes. The cauldron was an iron black obstacle forbidding passage to the unknown.

"I don't know if I want to do this anymore," said Natalie aloud as if she was trying to talk to someone. She held the protection pouch tight in her hands as she went and laid down on her bed. She pulled her blankets tight around her as a shield against the unknown that faced her.

Natalie was fast asleep clutching the pouch with her hands when she was awakened by a loud chime of a clock tower. "Oh," said Natalie.

Without thinking she quickly jumped to her feet off her bed and grabbed the box of matches. She lit the first match and held it to the wick of the left candlestick.

On the sixth chime Natalie struck the second match on the side of the box and held it down inside the small cauldron. The incense started to smoke and fill the room with a haunting aroma of musty air.

She waited and counted the chimes. At the eleventh chime of the tower clock she lit the last match and held it to the dark red bee's wax candle on the right.

Natalie sat down at her desk and placed her hands palms down on each side of the journal. It seemed the last chime was taking for ever to ring. "Did I miscount? Have I missed it?" thought Natalie.

Chapter Four
Witchcraft School

The room darkened except for the candlelight on the desk. Natalie looked around. All she saw was the musty smoke of the incense around her. There were echoed sounds off in the distance. She heard water dripping into a puddle with the echoed effect. Her skin crawled with goose bumps as the air was deathly still and damp.

"Is this her?"

Natalie heard the question without seeing who was asking.

A shadowed figure approached the desk. A man bent down to get a better look at Natalie. The flickering candlelight illuminated his face giving Natalie and uneasy feeling deep in her gut.

He had a long brown and gray beard with similar hair to match. He wore half spectacles that sat on the end of his nose. He gave a short smile to Natalie and said, "Shall we get started."

The room lit up with bright light from nowhere. The wizard was standing a few feet away from Natalie with a chalkboard next to him.

"Open you journal to the first page. Write on it what appears on the board."

Natalie looked up at the chalkboard. It had written on it 'Natee's shadow book of spells and potions'.

Natalie thought to herself, "Natee, hem, Natee the witch. It makes me sound like a good and caring person."

She opened the bottle of ink and picked up the quill and began to write. When she was done she sat down the quill and clasped her hands together.

Next to the wizard was a chalkboard that had on it the Thirteen Principles of Magic.

"On the next two pages write down the following," said the wizard.

Again Natalie looked up at the board. At the top she read, "The Thirteen Principles of Magic."

She began to write: The Thirteen Principles of Magic.

One, Magic cannot do unnatural effects.

Two, Physical magic must comply with nature's laws.

Three, Astral magic is limited to the plain in which you are in.

Four, Mental magic must be precise. Perception cannot use guesswork.

Five, Negative magic must not be mixed with negative emotions. Negative magic mixed with positive emotions obtains positive results.

Six, Positive magic has healing powers. Do not mix positive magic with negative emotions. The healing powers can destroy one's magical ability.

Seven, Timing must be exact when combining different magical effects for a single result.

Eight, Color of magic can be used in all forms of magic to give a positive spin on the end result.

Nine, Properties of nature's elements must be respected. Disfigurement of nature's elements will result in an imbalance and can cause uncontrolled magical effects.

Ten, Tools of magic have personalities, and must be taken in consideration when using them to do magic.

Eleven, Know the difference between creatures of magic and magical creatures.

Twelve, Defense against magic doesn't require overpowering magic. Clear thinking can drive away dark forces better than a magical sword.

Thirteen, Defense against non-magical forces. Resist using magic to remove the non-magical force as it will give it more power. The best defense is to ignore it.

Again Natalie set down her quill and clasped her hands together. After a minute or so she said, "Excuse me what does that all mean?"

The wizard turned around and said, "When asking a question start with 'Master Wizard Sir' then wait to be acknowledged before continuing."

Natalie sat there for a moment then said, "Master Wizard Sir?"

"Yes Natee, you have a question?" asked the wizard.

"Can you explain what the thirteen principals of magic mean?" asked Natalie.

"These are the principles that govern how magic works. We will go through each one to develop your magical skills," said the wizard.

"Master Wizard Sir?" asked Natalie.

"Yes Natee, you have another question?" said the wizard.

"What is the reason you had me write my name as Natee?" asked Natalie.

"That is the name your great, great grandmother named you when she first knew that you had the magical powers of a witch," said the wizard. "That is the name for which her magical amulet will respond to when it comes time for you to receive it. Now lesson one, principle one, magic cannot do unnatural effects. When doing magic, if you try to set water on fire when you know that water will quench fire this is considered an unnatural act of magic."

"Master Wizard Sir?" said Natalie.

"Yes Natee?" asked the wizard.

"I've seen magicians set water on fire. How is it that they can do it?" asked Natalie.

"Magicians do trickery, not magic. They are misnamed. To answer your question, they simply float an easy burning fuel on top of the water. It burns instead of the water," explained the wizard.

Witchcraft school went on for hours until morning had arrived. Natalie woke up in her bed with her hands holding the protection pouch.

"Was that all a dream?" she asked herself. She looked at her desk. The candlesticks had wax that dripped down the side from burning.

Natalie went over to the leather journal and opened it. On the first page was written 'Natee's Spell and Potion Journal'. She turned the page to see written there the thirteen principles of magic. On the next few pages were spells and potions she remembered that she had written down to help understand the first principle of magic.

Natalie's mom knocked on her door. "Natalie, are you awake?"

"Just a moment mom, let me finish getting dressed," said Natalie as she quickly closed the journal and grabbed the candles and cauldron. She pulled opened a clothes drawer and hid them under her underwear. Just as she was closing the drawer Melissa opened the door.

"You don't have to be embarrassed if you're not fully dressed," said Melissa. "Oh is this your school project?"

Melissa was looking at the leather book sitting on the desk. Natalie got between the leather book and her mother. "Yes it is. I uh bought this as a diary, to write about our trip to Broomstick. The project was to keep a journal for the summer. So I thought I would make it special. You know for extra credit," said Natalie. She knew that was a lie, but it wasn't a total lie.

Natalie pulled the leather strap around the book and tied it closed. "Can I help you make breakfast?" asked Natalie to avert her mom's attention away from the leather book.

Natalie sat in her room reading and re-reading what she had written in the journal. She was waiting for Mukul to return, but he never showed up. Again late at night she was awoken by the clock tower bell chime.

Natalie jumped out of bed and opened her drawer where she had hidden the candlesticks and cauldron. She had just gotten the first candle lit when the second bell chimed. Then she scurried to find the dragon blood incense and put a piece in the cauldron. Hoping that she counted right the incense was lit and smoking filling the room again with that musty air smell. Finally the last candle was lit and Natalie sat at her desk with her palms flat on top on each side of the journal.

The room once again darkened and the echo of dripping water was heard. The stone room illuminated and the wizard was standing there next to the chalkboard.

"Let's continue on. Principle two, Physical magic must comply with nature's laws. You cannot change objects into a different material then what it is made of. My example is that you cannot turn ice into diamonds. One can change the shape of ice. It can be made to look like a stone statue. But it will still melt just like ice," explained the wizard. "Now open your journal and we'll write a spell to turn wood into stone."

"Master Wizard Sir?" said Natalie.

"Ah, I anticipated your question. What nature has already has done, so magic can also do. Example is the petrified forest," said the wizard.

"No sir that was not my question," said Natalie.

"Oh, then what do you wish to ask, Natee," said the wizard.

"Is witchcraft school going to be like this every night? That is to say, at midnight I must light the candles and incense and

31

wait. I attend school during the weekdays. Then there is my parents, if they found out what I am doing they will take away everything. And Mukul hadn't returned to help me," asked Natalie.

"What you are doing is opening the portal to this room to come to class. If you are worried about getting enough sleep, I assure you, you are not missing any sleep time. You return back to your bed at the same time that you had left. In a sense we are stealing time."

"Isn't that considered against nature?" questioned Natalie?

"Ah this is a good example of the second principle. What we are doing is using a single second of time to do hours of study," said the wizard. "Now about your parents, they do not know that you are being tutored?"

"My parents wouldn't approve of any of this. I'm sneaking out at night, learning witchcraft from a wizard they don't even know," said Natalie.

"How strange, but why would they take away your magical equipment? Do they think you are too young? I'll have to discuss this with them before any more sessions can happen."

"Oh Master Wizard Sir, please don't talk to my parents. My mother wouldn't understand. She thinks that Mukul is a handmade raggedy stuffed toy that my great, great grandmother had given me. She isn't a witch."

"Well then I'll just speak to your father," said the wizard.

"My father isn't a wizard either," said Natalie. "I'm the only one that has any magical powers in my family."

"Oh, this is a difficult situation indeed. I must discuss this with Mukul. For right now we'll just finish the thirteen principles of magic. Every witch should know and understand them no matter what the circumstances are," said the wizard.

Under his breath the wizard said to himself, "This may be why I am to stay anonymous to her."

Chapter Five
It's Your Move

When one picks up dice and tosses them to see how many spaces they will move in a board game, they are held to chance. The same is in life when one makes a major change like quitting one's job and moving to a complete different town to start anew. You are under the control of random circumstances, or so one would think.

It was by complete chance that the 'Once in a Lifetime Job Opportunities' newsmagazine happened to come through the mail to Howard Keystone's place of employment. And it was just a lucky chance that he happened to be the only one to inquire into the property that was for sale in the town of Broomstick. Or could it be that only one member of the Keystone family has magical powers might have something to do with the whole situation? No, pure coincidence I'm sure.

Who would really gain from manipulating this one single family to move to the town of Broomstick? Roll the dice, it's your move.

Actually it is the Keystone's move. Howard convinced Melissa that they could back out of the deal if she didn't like it. They were just going there for a vacation and that was it.

"We'll play a game with this. Everyone will have a notepad and pen. Starting at the city limits each one of us will write down what we see and rate it if we like it or don't like and why," said Howard to his skeptical family.

"How will we know who won the game?" asked Fitzpatrick. "You're just asking for opinions."

"Okay, let's say if you have an opinion on your notepad that no one else has, you get ten points. And for every opinion that matches someone else you lose one point for every match, which could add up to a maximum of negative four points per opinion," quipped Howard.

Mukul hasn't been around since that first night of the witchcraft school. Natalie attended every night even after regular school had let out for the summer.

"Master Wizard Sir?" said Natalie.

"Yes Natee, you have a question?" said the wizard.

"No sir, I need to let you know that next week our family is going on vacation for the entire month of July. I can't attend school," said Natalie.

"That will be good because I will be finished with the thirteen principles of magic," said the wizard. "I won't be able to continue until I talk to Mukul about this situation."

Natalie liked witchcraft school and wished for it not to

stop. Mukul had told Natalie that her magical powers were not activated yet and were dormant inside her. She had discovered on her own since attending this special school that she had some limited magical powers she could use. She could do things that affected her.

Color magic enhanced her perception of what was around her. She could see things, or know something without having any knowledge of it before that moment. There was one matter that was coming clear to her that didn't take any magic to know. Her mother was getting suspicious. She hadn't said it yet but it won't be too much longer, Natalie believed, before she accused her of being what was most distasteful to Melissa's family tree.

Melissa hated that word. To her it was the worst Anglo-Saxon word that had survived centuries of language changes.

Natalie once overheard her mother talking to the air.

"My great grandmother was the last of their kind," said Melissa aloud to herself. "I will put a stop to this as soon as I figure out who is fanning the flames of this horrid practice."

It was during that moment it suddenly hit Melissa. The strange things with Natalie all started after she got rid of that shoebox in the backyard brick barbeque.

"What was that thing that Shasta gave Natalie?" All these years Melissa thought it was just a worn out handmade stuffed toy cat. "She was talking to someone, not to that toy!" she exclaimed.

Natalie wasn't sure about things anymore. Witchcraft school started well, but the midnight ritual of getting there was, to her point of view, very dangerous. If she was ever caught by her mother there would be more than just being grounded to pay for this. She had thoughts of being shackled to her bed with candles all around her. A self proclaimed holy man would be reciting gibberish while throwing purified water or some other less than desirable smelly concoctions on her.

"Det ska betala för den chateau tillflyktsorten som jag alltid har velat. (This will pay for that chateau retreat I've always wanted.)," said the self proclaimed holy man standing at the foot of the bed wearing a tall pointy hat with feathers sticking out in all directions.

"Natalie, Natalie!" her mother called out.

Natalie came out of her nightmarish daydream and look at her mother.

"Natalie are you all packed?" asked Melissa.

"Yes mom, I gave the suitcase to Dad," answered Natalie.

Natalie left behind the candlesticks and the cauldron with the dragon's blood incense. Out in plain view she carried her spell and potion journal. After all it was suppose to be a diary of their summer vacation.

Mukul still hasn't showed up since that first night of witchcraft school. Natalie was worried, more for herself, than for him. She had no direction.

Everyone was in the family size sport utility vehicle with Natalie stuck all the way in the back by herself in the seats that had little leg room and no way out. She made the best of it by being quiet and reading her journal. That last night of witchcraft school gave Natalie a cramp in her hand from all the writing. There were so many potions and spells that showed each of the thirteen principles of magic.

Her favorite spell was the one that showed how color magic enhanced all magic. "In a mortar and pestle crush rose petals of (select the color type depending on what powers are needed). Blend the crushed petals into white tea and brew. Drink slowly while listening to music. Pick one instrument and focus your attention on it. After the music is over turn out the lights, do your magic in the dark and see it all come to light."

Natalie sat in the back sipping the tea she had made earlier with crushed deep red rose petals and had her headphones over her ears listening to the ting of the symbol that kept the beat through the song. After it had finished playing she kept her eyes closed and focused her mind on the town of Broomstick. She was trying to do a virtual tour of the town.

She found herself on a quiet street void of vehicle traffic. It was late afternoon with the sun slowly drifting down into the top of various tree limbs that lined the street. The storefronts were odd, not like the normal strip mall storefronts in the city. And the names were quite different. They reminded her of when she was looking for the metaphysical shops for Mukul.

Natalie passed by all kinds of shops. There were clothing stores, potions supplies, antiquity stores, healing clinics, and clairvoyant parlors. These business establishments had unusual names. They were Astradom Obsession, Edna's Antiquities, and Big Bang Ariel Haven.

When Natalie got to the bright neon sign for Moonlite and Spiders Crossquarter Festival glow-in-the-dark supply store she gave it a quick glance.

The simple storefront sign across the street got Natalie's curiosity. It pulled at her as if someone was calling her name.

She read it aloud, "Hidden Quiddity Potion Shop."

It was nothing fancy. It didn't light up, blink, or sparkle. But a feeling drew Natalie toward the door. She crossed the street and stood in front of the door.

As she reached for the door it suddenly flung open inward. A man dressed in a dark green and yellow robe attempted to exit the potion shop.

"Excuse me young lady," Winston said politely.

Natalie stepped aside to allow him to leave. She caught the door and stood there looking inside. Up on the counter she saw Mukul standing there talking to a woman with dark hair cut to her jaw line.

Natalie let the door shut and stood on the sidewalk. Not understanding what she had seen, she just started walking. There was no direction or reason for where she was walking to.

Natalie passed an old florist shop that was closed and other empty storefronts in the same location. In the distance she saw the gates of the town cemetery. It was quiet and the grass was green.

Natalie held the iron fence while she pondered the view. Shadows were stretched out long from the sun setting low in the western sky. Without warning she felt the icy cold of a bony hand that grabbed her arm. She found herself staring into the hollow openings of a skull. Suddenly she inhaled a deep breath.

"Mom, something is wrong with Natalie. Her face is pale gray and I don't think she is breathing," said Fitzpatrick.

"Howard, pull over now!" yelled Melissa.

After the vehicle had stopped Melissa pulled opened the

back door and ordered the boys to get out. Then she moved the middle seat out of the way. She climbed into the back and grabbed Natalie's arm.

"Natalie, Natalie!" Melissa screamed as she shook Natalie.

Natalie's eyes opened wide as she took in a deep breath. Her color slowly started coming back to her face.

Melissa saw the plastic bottle that was next to Natalie and smelled the contents. "What was in this?" she demanded.

Natalie caught her composure and answered, "It was just some white tea that I brewed up." She left out the rose petal part of the ingredients.

Howard and Melissa stood away from their offspring at the gas station to talk quietly. "I'm telling you, the family would find great, grandmother the same way. She would be in a trance or something. It scared them to death."

"You're jumping to conclusions. Natalie may have had some reaction to the tea she drank, nothing more. I thought all that superstition nonsense stopped when your great grandmother died," said Howard.

"I won't be satisfied until I see that so called diary of hers that she is carrying around. If I am right, that is the same kind of strange book great grandmother carried close to her at all times," said Melissa.

"Didn't you say no one ever found that book?" asked Howard.

"Many things of hers disappeared after her death," stated Melissa. "But if I am right, that is no diary."

"I'm telling you, you're imagining things, and I'll prove it," said Howard.

Howard walked back to the car and asked Natalie, "What have you written in your diary so far?"

"Not much," said Natalie. "Just our destination."

"Could I see what you have written so far? Your mother is concerned that you might be writing crazy stuff," said Howard.

Natalie stood there with the journal clutched in her arms. If she refused, they would just force it from her.

"Okay, I'll let them read it. They can't stop me from being a witch. I'll just get another book," thought Natalie.

"Here, I'm not ashamed of what is in it," said Natalie.

Howard opened up the journal to the first page. Both he and Melissa stared at the words, "Natalie's trip to the town of Broomstick." On the next two pages was a list, "First thirteen reasons why I will like living in Broomstick."

Howard closed the book. "Well I've read enough. Melissa, are you satisfied?"

"I, um, I, well yes I guess so. I'm sorry. I'll just stop this nonsense," said Melissa as she walked over the passenger side of the car and got in. "Trickery, just like great grandmother."

"Here you go sweetie, just don't drink anymore tea, okay?" said Howard.

Natalie stood there with her journal. She looked inside at the first page, "Natee's shadow book of spells and potions."

She looked at her parents, shrugged her shoulders and climbed into the back seat. Natalie discovered her quill and ink may keep people from reading what she had wrote in her journal.

On her note pad she wrote with the quill everything she had

seen in the town of Broomstick on her virtual tour. She tried to capture every little detail, especially who Mukul was talking to in that potion shop.

"Well your directions said to turn left," said Melissa.

"Did you read the street name right?" asked Howard.

Natalie spoke up from the back seat. "The bakery is in the corner strip mall by the town's cemetery. Turn right at the next street and drive down two blocks. Moonlite and Spiders Crossquarter Festival glow-in-the-dark supply store will be on your left and the Hidden Quiddity Potion Shop will be on the right. Keep going for three more blocks and turn right again. It will be on your left side where all the empty storefronts are."

Howard followed Natalie's directions and pulled into the parking lot of the empty stores. "Why are they all closed or empty?" asked Melissa.

"It's haunted," said Natalie. "No one can keep a business here because of what goes on after the sun sets."

Both her brothers started laughing. "It haunted. OOOH, I'm scared mommy," said Donavan sarcastically.

"How do you know all this? How to get here and why these stores are out of business?" asked Howard.

Natalie didn't have an answer that didn't require her to lie. She just shrugged her shoulders with a questioned expression on her face.

Melissa looked back at her daughter with a firm look of

knowing the real answer. "You just knew. It came to you like you might have been here before or something."

Natalie looked away from her mother's stare. "Yeah, something like that," said Natalie as she slumped back behind the seats trying to hide.

Chapter Six
Stranger Things

Broomstick is located in the middle of the United States. While driving on the interstate, don't blink or you'll miss the sign for the exit to Shadow Creek Valley and Broomstick.

Here you will find the most influential families in the magical world. Some of those families are the Candlewicks, the McDermits, and the Wisestones. These families are connected in one way or another through blood and marriage.

Agnes and Harriet are the owners of the Hidden Quiddity Potion Shop. Their maiden name was Candlewick. Agnes is married to Franklin McDermit and Harriet is married (she prefers the old name of hand fasted) to Winston Wisestone.

Franklin is the Master Wizard of Broomstick. Winston is the Mayor of Broomstick and the caretaker of the strip mall with the bakery that Howard Keystone was interested in.

Franklin and Winston were having lunch at the Poison Apple Tavern while Agnes and Harriet were setting up their potion booth for the Renaissance Faire on the first weekend in July. Which happened to be the day the Keystones were arriving in Broomstick.

"I didn't even have the property listed anywhere. I'm still working on the cause of the nightly haunting of that strip mall. Out of the blue a call comes to me on my personal number from this guy that is answering an ad with my phone number on it. What do you make of that?" said Winston.

"That strip mall has been cursed ever since Zimmer Wardcrystal the Ghoul had anything to do with it. We missed something when we cleaned up his mess after we sent him off to the Underworld. There is still something in that storefront worse than that zombie we found in the crate that he must have kept hidden in a secret place," said Franklin.

"Just a year ago the Olsen family handed the deed to the ranch house and the strip mall over to City Hall and left town swearing they would never return," said Winston as he picked up a finger niblet, dipped it into a mustard and onion sauce. Winston took a bite.

"What are you going to tell these people?" asked Franklin as he sipped his rich foamy carbonated witch hazelnut soda through his beard. The foam circled around his mouth on his beard.

"There is nothing wrong with the ranch house and acreage. I told them they could stay there for the month for free. This is their vacation time," said Winston as he finished his batwing soup and wiped off his mouth. "I hate to eat in a rush but I am meeting them at one o'clock. Want to come along?"

"No, I have business to attend to with an old friend," said Franklin.

After looking through the dingy window of the bakery, the Keystone's headed to meet with Winston Wisestone at the ranch house, with a slight detour.

"Hey I know the three of you have been cooped up in the car and this meeting will be boring. So how about you start your vacation by going to the Broomstick Renaissance Faire. We'll meet up with you later at four o'clock at the entrance?" asked Howard.

Fitzpatrick, Donavan, and Natalie were dropped off at the front of the fair grounds. The two boys took off leaving Natalie standing there alone, which was just fine with her.

Natalie was still holding her spell and potion journal when she walked through the gate. Instantly her clothes changed from her sleeveless top and blue jeans to a vintage outfit of the renaissance era that consisted of a chemise, an outer skirt, a bodice, and a snood.

Natalie looked around to see if anyone noticed. Not a single person was gawking at her. "Good morrow," said the lady that was dressed similar as she handed Natalie an event program.

Natalie walked slowly looking at the retail booths and the people. One booth caught her eye. It carried stylish robes and witches hats with some fancy magic wands. Other booths had little dragons holding crystal balls or sticks of incense.

She passed the games where her brothers were busy throwing axes at wood targets. Farther down the majestic dirt road made a curve. There were some of the queen's guards and well dressed people. Natalie watched as they put on a skit of opening a section of the road in the name of the Queen.

She walked around the curve to see a woman yelling at people as they came by her booth. "Ello Govnor," said the woman. "Trouy me luv poshun?"

Natalie said to herself, "That is a very bad English accent."

Then the woman turned to face her. It was the woman in the Hidden Quiddity Potion Shop that was talking to Mukul.

Natalie walked near the booth to get a closer look at the woman. She took in a deep breath for courage and walked up to the booth. "Do you know where Mukul is?"

Harriet turned to the young girl and said with her bad accent, "Now you'd be jus a bit ta young for me luv poshun."

Natalie asked her question again. "Do you know where Mukul is?"

Harriet stopped her act and paid attention to Natalie. She viewed her for a moment then asked in her normal voice, "You wouldn't by any chance be Natalie?"

"Yes, I am Natalie. Now I answered your question, could you answer mine?"

"I really don't know," Harriet answered. "Natalie, I'm Harriet. Mukul told me you would be showing up. He just didn't exactly say where or when."

"How do you see Mukul?" asked Natalie.

"With my bewitching eyes," said Harriet with a little laugh.

"What I meant to ask was, do you see him as a cat or a stuffed toy," inquired Natalie.

"Oh, that is a queer question," said Harriet. "I don't know exactly how to answer you. That is to say I'm not sure you should know the answer."

Harriet opened a section of the booth to Natalie. "Why don't you come in and we'll talk."

After Natalie entered the booth, Harriet dropped the front cover down over the booth. "How is it that you know Mukul?"

Natalie thought about it for a moment then answered, "He is my familiar. My great, great grandmother Shasta passed him to me just before she passed away."

Harriet could not hold in her emotion after hearing this. She began to laugh, and laugh loud, and laugh hard.

"Ha ha ha, ho ho, hee hee, Ah ha ah ha ha ha!"

Her sides ached from laughing so much. In between breaths she said, "He's your familiar? Ah ha ah ha ha ha! Did he tell you that? Ha ha ha, ho ho hah hah."

"Well yes, sort of. He told me that he was my great, great grandmother's familiar and since she gave him to me that makes him my familiar," said Natalie not understanding why Harriet found this so funny.

"I will say that makes logical sense, but Mukul is a... Ha ha ha," Harriet stopped laughing.

What Harriet was about to say, set in. The situation became clear to her that this wasn't so funny anymore.

Franklin whisked away from the Poison Apple Tavern not long after Winston had left. Mukul was waiting for him at his wood shack high up in the mountains that he had lived in since his exile from the rest of the world.

The wind howled and the temperature was sub-zero high up on top of the mountain peak that rose over Shadow Creek Valley.

Mukul had a fire going in a black potbelly stove with a pan sitting on top inside a sturdy one room wood shack.

"Here have some coffee," said Mukul as he offered Franklin a porcelain mug.

"I couldn't tell you at first. I knew you wouldn't agree to the situation," said Mukul as he sipped the hot muddy coffee.

"How did you find her? I clearly don't understand how she could have magical powers and not her parents," said Franklin. He took a sip of the coffee and made a grimace expression.

"I didn't find her. She is the great, great granddaughter of Shasta," admitted Mukul.

"Magic skipped two generations? Do you have any idea what would cause that?" asked Franklin.

"It was Shasta herself that caused it. She actually thought she killed her magic with a spell that backfired," said Mukul still sipping his coffee.

"That was when I came into her life. You know my situation. It was through her magic I got this far," continued Mukul. "But the damage was done and her children didn't inherit any magic. They grew up thinking their mother was off her rocker. Her grandchildren were abusive with their comments behind her back."

"How horrible to live with magic and have no one to share it with," exclaimed Franklin who was sadly looking into his coffee mug.

"Her last years were made happy through little Natee. When she felt the magic in her, she knew she had an heir for her amulet. Shasta made me promise to guard her amulet until it was the right time to pass it on to Natee. I'm not ashamed that I have used it for my own personal gain," said Mukul as he gulped down the last of his coffee.

"What about the girl now, I can't allow her to be taught without her parents' permission. She would be sneaking out behind their backs again. This could get me in trouble with the conference," stated Franklin.

"If I get their permission will her tutoring continue?" asked Mukul.

"How are you going to do that? Don't deceive them with magic and deceive me as well with false documents," said Franklin.

"It will be legitimate, I assure you. I'll have it in writing for you soon," said Mukul.

Franklin set down his half drank coffee mug on the table. "I won't be needing it for another month. She went on a vacation with her family."

The two gave each other a hug and a pat on the back. "Remember the first rule of wizards, watch your back," said Franklin as he walked out of the wood shack and disappeared in the fog.

Mukul tighten his braded belt around his wizard robe and put on his wide brim hat. He picked his staff that held the amulet of Shasta in a globe held on by a hand carved dragon talon. Mukul stepped out of the wood shack and vanished with a flash of blue sparkles.

Chapter Seven
Baking up Terror

Winston just materialized behind the ranch house and was walking around to the front of the ranch house when the Keystone's drove up the gravel driveway from the main road. He was wearing normal attire that he would wear as Mayor. Winston wore a Düben Fashions designed business suit.

Winston was the first to speak up. "Welcome to Broomstick," he said with a smile and a hand out waiting for Howard to reach him at the front door.

"I had a cleaning crew come in and spot clean the house. It wasn't quite ready for occupants, but you and your children should be very comfortable here," said Winston walking them through the house.

Melissa was the first to notice how everything was spotless and polished in the kitchen. Even the cast iron skillet had a mirror like surface.

"I was noticing the landscaping on the way in. I've never seen such detail except at an amusement park," said Howard. "Didn't you say over the phone the property was a little rundown and needed work?"

51

"I assure you this look won't last long. I just wanted you to come here and have a nice vacation for your family," said Winston.

Melissa whispered to Howard, "He's going to up the price. This is a setup, just you watch."

"Well here are the keys to the door. If you need anything just call this number," said Winston as he handed them a business card and the keys.

Winston walked out the front door where a car was waiting. Melissa called out, "Mr. Wisestone, how about coming by for dinner? Mr. Wisestone?"

Winston was in the car and drove off not hearing Melissa calling out to him. Melissa didn't see the car disappear once it reached the main road.

Melissa turned to Howard, "I don't like this. There is something strange going on here. The strip mall is empty and in shambles, but this place is manicured to perfection. And where did Mr. Wisestone drive off to so quickly?"

"Melissa please, let's just enjoy our vacation. I'm sure all our questions will be answered in time," said Howard. "How about a quick swim in the pool then we'll go and pick up the kids?"

"Where is your sister? Why isn't she here with you?" yelled Melissa.

"We saw her go into one of the booths with a woman and she never came out," said Fitzpatrick.

"Take me to this booth!" demanded Melissa.

The boys led the way as their mother followed through the

crowd of faire goers. "This one," said Fitzpatrick as he pointed to the booth with the cover pulled down.

Melissa pulled up the cover and climbed over the counter. There was no one in the booth at all. It didn't take security long to show up.

"Hey you, you're not allowed to enter the booths," said one security officer.

"My daughter came in here with a woman and never came back out. I want to know who this booth belongs to and where she has taken my daughter!" said Melissa not backing down from searching the rest of the booth.

On the outside of the booth Natalie made her way to the front of the crowd. "Dad, what is Mom doing? I saw you at the front of the faire and tried to catch up to you."

"Melissa, Natalie is out here with us," said Howard.

"Where have you been and who is this woman you were with?" yelled Melissa.

Security stepped in, "Come this way and we'll work all this out."

The Keystone's were escorted to an area out of the view of the faire goers. "Calm down and we will find out who this woman is."

"Mom, I was with Harriet Wisestone. Her husband is Winston Wisestone the Mayor. And if you only waited a few more minutes you could have met her. Instead I was running through the crowd trying to catch up with you. Only if Mukul was here," said Natalie.

Melissa asked, "What did you say?"

The security officer interrupted before Natalie had to answer her mother.

"Is this your daughter?" asked a security officer.

Howard answered, "Yes officer, this is our daughter. There had been a meeting time error."

"If we are free to go we'll just leave and not cause any more trouble," said Melissa. "I'm sure we can resolve any differences with the Wisestone's outside of here."

"Alright, there is a way out over here from the faire," said the security officer.

Melissa stared at Natalie with razor sharp eyes. She change her voice and said, "Yes that will be fine. I'm sorry officer for causing a scene."

At the ranch house Melissa motioned to Natalie to go to one of the bedrooms. She closed the door behind the two of them. "Now who is Mukul?" asked Melissa with a stern voice.

Natalie just stood there and stared around the room avoiding any eye contact with her mother.

"Alright I'll tell you who I think this Mukul is. It was that stuffed toy that your great, great grandmother gave you. Only it was not just a stuffed toy was it? It talked to you, or so you think it did. Shasta was the same way. She talked to herself too saying she was talking to someone else," said Melissa as she circled around the room.

Natalie just stood there not looking at her mother.

"Does this voice tell you to do strange things? Let me give you some examples of what your great, great grandmother did. She would light candles in the middle of the night, burn incense in a cauldron, and chant gibberish while waving a carved stick in the air. In other cauldrons the making of liquids boiled without any fire under them. She would drink them. That was when the family would find her ashen and almost not breathing, just like you were. Did the voice of this Mukul tell you to drink poison?" Melissa was not through yet. She kept pacing around Natalie who was still trying to ignore her.

"Another thing your great, great grandmother would do was to take black cats and cut their throats and drank their blood on Halloween," said Melissa with a nasty smile.

"That's a lie. Grandma Shasta was a good witch. She never did any black magic. She healed and helped people. You, all of you shunned her for what she could do. Her magic wasn't passed down to any of you. So you resented her. She saw that I had the magic and gave me Mukul to protect me from you. Now he is helping me to become a witch just like her," screamed Natalie while tears rolled down her face. "I am going to be a witch and you cannot stop me because it has already started. If you want me to do black magic I will. I swear I will."

Natalie pointed her finger at her mother and said, "Get out of my room and never set foot in here ever again in anger at me."

Melissa walked backward to the door and fumbled for the doorknob. She got the door opened and pulled it shut as she left.

Natalie dropped to her knees. She held her hands over her face and cried hard. "Mukul where are you? I just messed up everything."

Winston stood in front of the bakery shop that was two stores down from where Zimmer Wardcrystal had his hideous chamber of horrors that he and Franklin had the pleasure of cleaning up. But they missed something.

First the card and novelty went out of business. The florist kept in business as long as he could, but the one wall soon grew so grotesque no one would come in.

Then just barely a year ago the Olsen's left not giving any reason as to why. The bakery still had the last baked items rotting in the display cases.

"I don't know what you are, but you will be exorcised from this place and sent to the center of a black hole never to escape into this universe again," shouted Winston.

The ground shook and the sidewalk began to roll. Two glowing eyes of intense hot colors appeared. They were the size of two storefront windows.

"Come and get me if you dare. I will eat your soul for a midnight snack and spit out your worthless skeletal bones for stray dogs to chew on."

"Don't threaten me with hollow attacks, you haven't any power that magic can't destroy," exclaimed Winston as he turned away from the windows and blazed a streak into the sky.

"I can't believe I let it get me angry like that," said Winston. He was sitting in a booth with his wizard friends having a mug of ale. "Tonight though, tonight I will exterminate it!"

"Not so fast," said one of his friends. "Don't go in there vengeful, remember principle number five. If you try to do magic against it you'll never come out. How about we help you figure out what this thing is first."

"I have only a month to do this. Howard Keystone has told me that he wanted to surprise his whole family at the end of the month that they're here to stay. He hasn't told them that he has already quit his job," said Winston.

"Well then let's get to baking up some terror and boil this thing in ghoul's blood," said another wizard.

They picked up their mugs and Winston reluctantly follow suit. "Cheers!"

The sun had just set when Winston and the other wizards arrived at the strip mall. Everything was dark and quiet. Winston unlocked the door to what was Zimmer Wardcrystal's ghoulish shop of horrors.

"What are we actually looking for?" asked one of the wizards.

"A secret room or compartment, somewhere to hide things," said Winston. "Franklin and I went through this store. We thought we took care of everything. We missed something. So it has to be hidden."

"Oh my, this old mop bucket reeks of pungent creatures," said another wizard.

"Just pour it down that drain grate," said Winston.

As the wizard poured the grungy water down the floor drain, it slowly backed up to just above the grating. Then the water began to churn and boil giving off an awful stench. Steam rolled out of the floor drain filling the room with a foggy atmosphere. Each wizard felt something drag across their skin like salty seaweed with sand.

"GET OUT OF HERE," yelled Winston.

The wizards exited through the front door into the deserted parking lot as tongues of fire lick their back sides. "Where's Winston? Winston!" one of the wizards yelled. He was heading back toward the door, but the other two wizards grabbed him and held him down to the ground.

The entire strip mall was covered with fog and smelled of rank garbage. It was in the early hours of the morning before the three wizards finally gave up any chance of re-entering the haunted store.

"We have to go and tell Harriet," said a wizard.

Harriet wasn't sleeping well with Winston not there. She was up making a cup of hot tea when a knock on the door disturbed the early morning quiet.

Harriet opened the door to find the three wizards standing at her front door.

"We're sorry Harriet," said the one wizard.

"There was nothing we could do," stated the second wizard.

"He saved us by telling us to get out just before the flames engulfed the inside of the store," explained the third wizard.

Harriet dropped her cup of tea. The cup shattered into a million shards of porcelain. "My Winston... Dead? No, I won't believe it until I see for myself," said Harriet with her fists clenched tight.

Kizee woke up when she heard the crash of the porcelain cup.

"I need you to go and stay with Gracie and George for a while. Something has happened to your Father," said Harriet to Kizee.

"What happened? Why can't I come?" questioned Kizee with high emotions.

"I'll come and get you later. Just do what I ask," said Harriet.

Harriet with the three wizards went to the strip mall. The whole area was blanketed by an orange glowing fog. It was too thick to navigate through to find the door of the insidious ghoulish store.

"There is nothing we can do here until we get some magical supplies," said one wizard.

Harriet didn't go home. Instead she went to the potion shop and hid in the reading room and cried herself to sleep in a chair.

It was just before nine in the morning when Agnes arrived at the Hidden Quiddity Potion Shop to find Harriet in the reading room.

"What are you doing here?"

"Winston is…" Harriet began to cry.

"Winston is what?" asked Agnes feeling something is not right.

"Winston is dead. He went to the strip mall and…" Harriet went back to crying.

Chapter Eight
The Mark of a Dead Man

It was a deep dark secret that Mukul kept within. He would have rather died on the altar of blood at the witch's council and taken this secret to the grave than to tell anyone what really took place.

It was early dawn in the village of Camden. The local authority had outlawed healing practices by other than the chief physician of the village. A little girl was lying in her straw stuffed bed with hand woven blankets wrapped around her. She had 'The Fever'.

Many had already died of this burning inflection in the village. The cause of their deaths was not the disease, it was the attempts to cure them.

The people of Camden use to rely on a wizard for their cures, until the day came when magic was outlawed and the new government established their ways of tending for the sick.

The village council appointed Tanaka Drake as chief physician. His style of healing was without merit. He was an experimenter.

His first case of 'The Fever' was with a middle aged man that was in good health until he took sick. Drake had his assistants carry the man into a boat and rowed out in the late night on the icy waters of the lake that was fed by the mountain glacier. The sick man was held in the water until his lips turned blue. He never regained conscious and died.

The next few cases Drake had them buried in cold mud up to their neck. When they began to shiver, Drake's assistants would dig them up only to rebury them the next day in a grave.

Then Drake started the bloodletting practice of bleeding out the disease from the sick person. They also died.

The villagers were fed up with Drake's tactics of torture. A spokesperson was chosen at a late night meeting held in secret. "We need our wizard back. He is the only one that can help us," said one woman who lost her only son to Drake.

"My daughter is sick with the fever and I will not let that mad man come near her. I want the wizard."

Mukul lived at the edge of town near the forest. Since the authorities outlawed the practice of magic, he kept to himself. It was very late in the night when a knock came on his door.

"I need your help," said the man. "My daughter, she has the fever."

"And you want me to break the law and cure her? Is my life worth less than your daughter's?" asked Mukul.

"Please I'm begging you, don't let my child fall victim to this mad man. You are our only hope," said the man.

Mukul already knew what he must do. He also knew the consequences of his actions. "If I help you, then in turn you and the rest of the village must help me."

"Yes, yes whatever you say. We will do what you want," begged the man knowing full well that it wasn't true.

The little girl was lying in her straw stuffed bed with hand woven blankets wrapped around her. Others as well as her parents were in the room. Mukul pulled from his rucksack a bottle and pulled the cork stopple out.

With his finger he rubbed the ointment on her forehead while chanting a spell.

"Farquest, bezellonus, yetella. Begone from this one and inflect no other. Nor sister, nor brother or father." Then he whispered into the girl's ear, "Sleep eternally my sweet. With you this disease also dies and will never kill anyone again."

Mukul continued to dab and rub the ointment on the girls head and face. Without warning Drake and his henchmen broke down the door and began to stab villagers with their sabers until they were standing over Mukul and the girl.

"I knew you couldn't keep to the law, sorcerer. It was just a matter of time," said Drake.

Mukul didn't resist arrest. He went quietly. The girl laid still in her straw bed. She was dead.

The word spread quickly that it was the wizard that had killed the little girl not the fever, and not Drake. There was a quick trial and Mukul was found guilty of performing healings and the murder of the girl. He was to be hanged by the neck until dead.

The night before the hanging Mukul walked out of his jail cell and disappeared.

It wasn't too long after that the magical governing body known as the witch's council heard of the death of a girl by a wizard. They wanted to know the truth.

Mukul was captured without any trouble. He stood before a

panel and heard what they had heard. "Is it true, you murdered this child to start a revolt against the local authority?"

Mukul put up in his defense the practices of Tanaka Drake chief physician of the village. "He is the murderer of this village. I was merely trying to save the lives of the next generations to come when I was interrupted in doing my spell. I take full responsible for my actions under their law. I shouldn't have broken the law and practiced healing."

On the morning of a total eclipse in land of Ugarit, Mukul was tied down on the stone table. The judge read the charge against Mukul for trying to start a revolution in the name of magic.

"Not guilty," yelled Mukul after the charge was read. Only he knew what he was really guilty of, and he was going to take that secret to his death.

"Wait, before you impose sentence hear me out," said a woman that just appeared in the witch's circle. "I am Euphoria a witch that lives in Camden. The villagers had already planned the revolt. They waited until that girl was near death before asking for Mukul's help. They used him as the match to light the fuse. His life should be spared for he did only what he knew was right." The woman hung her head and cried while the sentence was read.

The judge called the others of the council together. He then spoke with a booming voice. "It is the council's decision that you Mukul should live in torment of your deeds until you are vanquished by a pure hearted act. Your amulet will be crushed into shards and the smallest piece will remain with you. The rest of your amulet will be placed in the Realm of Forbidden Magic.

"No, just kill me,' yelled Mukul. "I'm guilty, I'm guilty, I'm guiltyeeeeee."

The shard of his amulet cut deep into the palm of his left hand leaving a scar in the shape of an eight legged spider for all to see. It wasn't going to be easy to live forever as a marked wizard with very limited magical power.

"Why did you save me, I was ready to die. I did what no wizard should ever do," Mukul cried.

His tears were hard and made a sound as they hit the wood floor of his shack. "I took a soul of a child."

"She was already dead. You knew that. No healing spell could have spared her life. But you save that whole village from that sickness by killing it then and there," said Euphoria. "The council has given you a second chance. Seek it out. Find this pure hearted act whoever it is. Most likely they will find you."

"Of course you are right, they will find me. I just have to have the courage to wait," said Mukul.

Mukul sat in his shack just for a moment after Franklin had left remembering what Euphoria had said centuries ago. He stood up and tightened his braded belt around his wizard robe and put on his wide brim hat. He picked up his staff that held the amulet of Shasta in a globe held by a hand carved dragon talon. Mukul stepped out of the wood shack and vanished with a flash of blue sparkles.

Mukul appeared outside of an unscrupulous dingy building that didn't have any windows in a realm that time had forgotten. Mukul opened the only door of the building and entered. Six Time Bandits were waiting for Mukul inside.

Mukul sat down in the only empty chair in the room. It was a very uncomfortable chair.

"For the last century you have asked for more time. What is your excuse this time wizard?" asked one of the Time Bandits.

"It's the same excuse that has plagued me this whole time, except this time I have put into motion my plan to get the information to retrieve the Hourglass of Time. I need another advancement on the money you're willing to pay me for the hourglass."

"This will be the last advancement. You've have spent almost half of our agreed price."

"Yes, yes I understand. I am very close in finding the opening to the outside of the universe. I will have the hourglass as promised," said Mukul.

It was the next morning Mukul appeared in front of Natalie once again as the cat. Natalie was still dressed in her clothes from the night before lying on her bed crying.

"What has your brothers done this time that the protection charm didn't stop?" ask Mukul as he stood in front of Natalie as the black cat.

"I've ruined everything. My mother figured out that I'm becoming a witch and I threatened her with black magic. They will lock me away in one of those asylums where they put disturbed people. She called grandma Shasta crazy and that she heard voices. And she said the same thing about me," said Natalie.

"Not to worry little one, together we will fix the damage. We are among friends here in Broomstick. This morning I want to take you somewhere to meet a witch. Her name is Harriet," said Mukul.

"I've met Harriet already. She told me who you are. You're not my great, great grandmother's familiar. You are a wizard that can't do very much magic at all," said Natalie.

"If you know the truth of who I am, it doesn't make any sense to stand here as a cat does it," said Mukul.

With a flash of blue light the small black cat vanished and standing in its place was a wizard wearing a brown robe and a large brimmed hat holding a staff.

"What will my family see you as now, a handmade wizard doll?" asked Natalie.

Mukul laughed. "No, that won't be necessary. I won't be hidden anymore. What do you say we take a trip and see our friend Harriet?"

"Sure, I can't be in any more trouble than I am in now," said Natalie.

"Hold on to my robe," said Mukul.

Melissa heard Natalie in her room talking to someone as she usually does. She stood at the door and listened. It was after a flash of blue light she observed from under the door that she heard a second voice.

Just about the time that Natalie said she would leave with this other person, Melissa had enough. "I'm going to break up this little party."

That was when a swirl of air blew from under the door at her feet as she opened the door. Natalie wasn't in her room and the window was still locked from the inside.

Natalie and Mukul appeared at the door of the Hidden Quiddity Potion Shop just minutes after Agnes arrived.

Natalie remembered standing at this door when she did her virtual walk around the town. Mukul pushed the door open and allowed Natalie to go into the potion shop.

"Wow, this is far better than that little Celestial Encounters metaphysical shop. This is the real deal," said Natalie.

She saw the drawers behind the counter marked magic wands. "When do I get to use a magic wand?"

"In good time, young one, in good time. I have a special one for you when the time comes," said Mukul.

Mukul heard Agnes and Harriet in the back of the potion shop. He found Agnes holding Harriet tightly. Mukul knew something was deathly wrong by the expressions on their faces. "I sense something dreadful has happened."

"Winston and three of his friends went after the creature that has plagued that strip mall over by the cemetery. He didn't make it out," said Agnes as she and Harriet sat in the reading room where Agnes' crystal ball sat.

"Has anyone gone back in to try to find him?" asked Mukul.

"The entire area is blanketed in an orange fog. Only death is waiting inside for anyone that enters," said Agnes.

Harriet sat there weeping and moaning "My Winston."

Natalie could only stand there and take in the situation. It occurred to her that the family's vacation is over. Her mother will want to leave as soon as possible, especially after she finds out about this tragedy where the bakery was. And with good timing, she heard her mother.

"Natalie? I know you're here," said Melissa with a loud voice coming from the potion shop.

"I'll handle this," said Mukul. "You stay here."

Mukul walked out to the front of the shop. "Hello Melissa."

"You? You should be long dead by now. You can't be over a hundred and fifty years and still alive," said Melissa.

"Oh I'm much older than that. It's good to see you again too," said Mukul. "Although I really had been in your family's presence for quite some time watching over Natalie."

"It was you that had been filling her mind with this foolishness. I thought we bred that ancient mythical practice out of our family tree. Natalie will not be one of your witches!" screamed Melissa.

"Stay here with Harriet," said Agnes to Natalie.

Agnes came out from the back room to see what the commotion was all about. "Is there something I could help you with?"

"Do you work here?" asked Melissa.

"I am the owner of this potion shop," replied Agnes.

"Then does Harriet Wisestone work for you?" inquired Melissa.

"She is my sister. Why do you ask?"

"She has been filling my daughter's mind with all this foolishness," said Melissa as she waved her hands around the shop.

Natalie burst out from the back room to face her mother. "No one is filling my mind with foolishness. Magic is real. What grandma Shasta did was real. And what I'm about to do is real."

Natalie pointed a magic wand that she picked up from the back room at her mother. Mukul quickly grabbed her hand and took the wand away.

"Stop, right now. I said I would handle this. You are letting your adolescence temper control your actions. And Melissa, you are letting your prejudices control your actions," said Mukul.

"Natalie, you're coming home with me right now. There will be no more of this nonsense," said Melissa.

"No, I'm not coming. I'm staying right here where I belong," retorted Natalie.

"No, Natalie. Go with your mother for now. Melissa, we'll sit down later and have a nice quiet talk. For now Natalie will not do any magic that you do not approve of," said Mukul.

"I approve none of this. Let's go Natalie," said Melissa.

Just before Melissa walked out the door, she turned back and pointed at Agnes. "And keep your sorceress sister away from my daughter."

Chapter Nine
Wesley Candlewick

"I thought you didn't know Mukul," said Natalie.

"I never knew his name. If I had known, that stuffed toy would have never been given to you," said Melissa. "I want you to stop this witchcraft nonsense. It is nothing but trouble. You'll find out it is all trickery and mind games."

Natalie didn't want to argue with her mother. If she even mentioned the portal to her witchcraft school or the virtual tour spell she would go berserk.

When they got back to the ranch house, Natalie's prediction was square on the money.

"We're leaving. This vacation is over, "said Melissa to Howard. "This is not the kind of small town I want to ever live in."

Natalie wanted to say, "I'm staying." But she knew that would only flame the argument.

Howard didn't move from his easy chair nor did he put down the local newspaper. "We can't leave. Part of the deal for getting to stay here for free was to allow someone from Broomstick to use our house for the same time period."

"You're telling me there are people from here in our house touching our things?" inquired Melissa.

"Winston assured me that nothing will be broken or out of place when we get back," said Howard.

Melissa stood there steaming. "Well fine then. I'm going shopping."

After some time had passed Natalie went to talk to her father. "Dad, something awful has happened where the bakery is. Winston Wisestone was trying to get rid of a poltergeist that plagued the strip mall. He may have been killed and the whole area is blanketed in an orange fog."

"You know for a minute you had me going. That was pretty funny. Although you shouldn't joke about someone dying," said Howard.

"I'm not making this up. Harriet Wisestone may be a widow, and your plans for opening the bakery will not happen," said Natalie.

"Okay, Natalie. Whatever you say," said Howard as he turned the page of his newspaper.

"Oh fine," said Natalie as she stomped off to her room.

Natalie closed the door and stood there with her arms crossed leaning up against the door. She noticed lying on her bed was her spell and potion journal opened to the pages with the thirteen principals of magic with a note from Mukul. "Study principal number five."

As Natalie sat on her bed looking at her journal a tapping noise on her window caught her attention. In the window was a boy's face that had silver blond hair, dark green eyes, and a square chin smiling at her. To Natalie he looked to be about her age.

Natalie opened the window just far enough to ask, "Why are you tapping on my window?"

"I wanted to meet you," said the boy.

"Then why didn't you just knock on the front door?" asked Natalie.

"Oh that would be awkward and embarrassing with a bunch of introductions and the such. I figured this was easier, you know just you and me," said the boy.

"Okay, so who are you?" asked Natalie.

"I'm Wesley Candlewick. I live across the road. I saw you at the Renaissance Faire today," said Wesley.

"Which time, the morning or the late afternoon when we were escorted away by security?" asked Natalie feeling a little embarrassed.

"Actually both times, I was moving potion supplies behind the potion booth when you came to talk to Harriet. I'm sort of related to Agnes and Harriet," explained Wesley.

When Natalie heard the boy say he was related to Agnes and Harriet she perked up and said, "I'll meet you out front of the house."

Natalie walked out of her room quietly. She went down the hall past the den where her father was still reading the newspaper. Quickly she turned the doorknob and opened the door. Once outside Natalie pulled the door closed without any noise. Wesley was standing right there on the porch.

"Come on let's go for a walk," said Natalie "Do you do magic?"

"I do some. Dad has a restriction charm around me," said Wesley.

"Are you a witch?" asked Wesley.

"I'm learning to be one. My magic is mostly dormant, but I have done some color magic," answered Natalie. "By the way, my name is…"

Natalie stopped and quickly thought, "This would be a good time to change her name."

"…Natee, Natee Keystone"

Wesley held out his hand and they both shook hands. "Hello Natee Keystone. Hey the sun's about to go down. Do you want to go and collect green sunset flash?"

Now Natee had no idea what Wesley was talking about. She knew of the phenomenon when the sun's rays bounced through the atmosphere off the curved surface of the ocean water. It appeared to flash green light at sunset.

"Uh, okay sure. You'll show me how, won't you?"

Wesley held out his hand again, this time though it was for them to hold hands. It was like a small thunder bolt clap when the two disappeared.

When they arrived at their destination, Natee fell to her hands and knees. She vomited up the turkey leg and the handmade ice slushy that she had eaten at the Renaissance Faire.

"Sorry, I guess I took off a little too quick,' said Wesley.

Natee picked herself up and wiped her eyes clear. "That's okay, I actually enjoyed it."

Wesley handed her a potion bottle with a special funnel shaped tip. "You look for the tree leaves that are twisted with a green glowing drop at the end. Put the tip of the potion bottle up to the drop, and then tap the leaf. When the drop falls into the bottle, the leaf will untwist."

They sat on a rock together as the sun went down not saying a word. The edge of the sun wavered in the atmosphere just before it melted away. The green flash danced over their heads in wavy streaks then cooled into the night air.

Wesley pulled Natee off the rock and straight over to a small tree. "Now watch, see the leaf start to twist. That is what we are waiting for."

The two of them hopped and skipped from tree to tree gathering the green liquid in their potion bottles. Natee's bottle was almost full when she asked the one question that didn't come to mind earlier because of all the fun she was having. "What does it do?"

"Stick out your tongue under this drop," said Wesley. He tapped the leaf and the green glowing drop of sunset flash hit Natee's tongue like an electrical spark.

"It tastes like cinnamon toast with extra butter," said Natee.

Then the real effect of ultra-happiness ran through her. She smiled with a wide grin.

"I feel like this night should never end." She grabbed Wesley and kissed him. "I'm sorry, I was so happy I couldn't help myself. You are the first person my age that I have met that can do real magic. Um, do you have a girlfriend?" asked Natee.

"No, that is kind of why I wanted to meet you when I saw you at the faire," said Wesley. "I wanted us to be friends."

Natee was blushing, still feeling the happiness from the flash drop. "We can be just friends if you like."

"Kissing friends?" asked Wesley

"Kissing friends," said Natee.

It was just before sunrise when Natee got back home to the ranch house. What she found there made her feel nauseous with a high fever. At first she thought it was the transindigitation back to her home. Then maybe it was the sunset flash wearing off. Or that she hadn't eaten anything in quite a while. No it was without a doubt what she found waiting for her at home.

There were broken broom sticks hanging in the trees, a large laurel branch wreath hanging on the front door with bay leaves scattered all over the front porch and the surrounding area.

Natee was getting dizzy. She began to slump down on the porch while trying to hold on to the railing. Her breathing became harder as she gasped for air. Melissa opened the door about the same time Mukul was walking up to the porch.

"You wretched woman, look what you have done. Who's doing black magic now?" said Mukul as he picked up Natee into his arms and started to walk away from the house.

"Where are you taking her?" yelled Melissa.

"Somewhere safe until she recovers from your voodoo," said Mukul. "I suggest you clean up your mess before it gets any worse."

Mukul carrying Natee walked across the road and knocked on the door.

"I hate to impose upon you, Mrs. Candlewick. But Natalie…"

Mukul was interrupted by a sick but alert girl. "Natee, (as she wheezed) my name is Natee."

"As I was saying, I hate to impose upon you. But Natee has become ill with laurelyngitis. Her mother was attempting to ward off the local witchery from coming around."

"Oh, please bring her in. Wesley was telling me about their fun activity of collecting sunset flash just before he went up to bed," said Katee Candlewick.

Mukul laid Natee down on the couch. "You'll start breathing better in a few minutes."

"How come you are not sick?" asked Natee.

"Oh, centuries of putting up with this mockery and practicing principal number thirteen," said Mukul.

"Here dear, drink this," said Katee.

Natee leaned up on one elbow and took a sip of the warm broth. "You must be Wesley's mother. I can tell by your beautiful hair. You're not angry with him that we stayed out all night are you?"

"Oh my no. Collecting sunset flash is an acceptable activity in Broomstick for kids your age. There is more than enough adults around collecting flash to keep a close eye on what you kids are doing," said Katee.

"A close eye? I didn't see anyone else out there," said Natee. Both Mukul and Katee laughed and smiled.

"Drink your broth. I'll be back shortly," said Mukul.

When Mukul showed back up he thanked Katee Candlewick for the hospitality and escorted Natee to the other side of the road. "I'll be showing up later to talk to your parents. In the meantime stay in your room, don't eat anything that your mother has made. And get some sleep."

When Natee arrived home, the troubles started all over again.

Melissa started yelling at her, "Who was that boy you stayed out all night with?"

Natee just walked to her room without saying anything to her mother.

"I'm talking to you young lady?" yelled Melissa.

Natee shut her door and plopped onto her bed. Although there wasn't a lock on the door, Melissa couldn't open it. Natee held her protection pouch in her hands and fell to sleep.

Chapter Ten
A Letter from the Grave

It was without a doubt the worst night in Harriet's life. Death never comes easy to accept. Even a witch with magical powers can feel helpless to change what has happened.

Agnes felt no different. Her experience didn't have any solution to the situation at the strip mall.

Many wizards including Franklin took turns in the vigil of watching for any change to the orange fogged area.

Agnes showed up with some hot soup while Franklin stood his watch in the late morning hazy sunrise. "What was that thing?" Agnes asked without expecting an answer.

Franklin sipped his soup. "That ghoul Zimmer Wardcrystal had the most horrific creatures that the dark side of nature could conjure up. Who knows what it could have been except another ghoul?"

"Let's not bring that two-faced wizard ghoul McKay into this. That would certainly make things worse," said Agnes.

The sky began to lighten as sunrise was creeping up to eliminate the cold nocturnal part of life. The orange fog scattered the sun rays in all directions not letting any penetrate into its depts.

A late morning breeze began to stir. Agnes and Franklin noticed the fog began to move. The bottom layer swirled upward in a circular pattern, while the upper layer spun like little tornados. The orange glow dimmed to a light gray then to translucent.

"Can you see anything?" asked Agnes as she squinted her eyes to lessen the sun's reflection off the fog.

"It appears to my eyes that there is nothing there," said Franklin as he took a step forward toward the fog. As the fog disintegrated, he would take another step closer. With his wand out in front at the ready to affix a protection spell, Franklin entered what was left of the dew forming misty fog.

By early noon the fog had disappeared. The strip mall was burnt to the ground. Only a few smoldering embers remained. Winston's charred body, or any fragment thereof was not to be found.

"I'm sorry Agnes, there isn't even one shred of hair to bury," said Franklin.

By midafternoon there was a line of mourners that stretched for blocks. They walked by the burned out strip mall laying flowers and lighting candles. All cried at the site. Harriet stood at the burned out site refusing her sister's pleas to leave. Agnes brought her sister some food. "At lease eat something."

Harriet's hair hung limped and her eyes were bloodshot from crying. By mid afternoon Harriet gave in to her sister. "Agnes I want to move back in to the potion shop. I can't go home anymore."

"The potion shop is still our first home. Just don't shut yourself inside," said Agnes.

It was midday when Mukul knocked on the ranch house door. Howard was the one that answered the door. He was looking at a strangely dressed man holding a staff with a clear glass ball embedded in a claw on the top.

"Good day Mr. Keystone, my name is Mukul. I need to talk to you and your wife about your daughter's future."

"Don't let him in," yelled Melissa from behind Howard.

"Mr. Keystone, your wife knows who I am. I was a friend of Shasta, her great grandmother. I am a wizard. This is very important. Natalie needs my help," said Mukul.

"She needs help alright, but not from you," said Melissa still standing in the far back behind Howard echoing down the hall.

"Mr. Keystone, please allow me to come in and sit down and discuss the matter with you. Melissa made a grave mistake last night that almost killed Natalie," said Mukul.

"Don't let him in. He doesn't know what he is talking about," said Melissa.

"This sounds pretty important. You don't have to talk to this man if you don't want to, but I want to hear what he has to say," said Howard over his shoulder.

Mukul accepted Howard's gesture to come in. He made his way to the living room and sat down in a comfortable chair. Howard followed by sitting down in the matching chair next to it. Melissa stood in the doorway of the living room.

"You said that Melissa made a grave mistake that almost killed Natalie," said Howard.

"Melissa hung in the trees broken broom sticks, placed a laurel branch wreath on the front door, and scattered bay leaves around the porch. When Natalie arrived home early this morning, she was exposed to the deadly toxic fumes that are given off from these objects," said Mukul. "I was appointed by Shasta to protect Natalie from her family, and I did just that by removing her from your house until Melissa cleaned up her mess."

"I don't understand. Broken broom sticks, laurel branches, and bay leaves aren't toxic?" said Howard.

"Not to you there not, but to a witch that is not properly schooled in warding off these non-magical forces, they are as deadly as if you poured rat poison down her throat," explained Mukul.

"But Natalie isn't a witch," said Howard.

"Yes I am," said Natee who was standing behind her mother being very quiet.

"Don't ever say that word in my house," said Melissa. "Go back to your room, Natalie."

"It's Natee for now on." Natee pushed by her mother into the living room. "If it wasn't for Mukul I would have died on the front porch this morning. I need to learn to be a witch with proper tutoring."

"You are not going to teach her anything," said Melissa.

"You finally said something we both agree upon. Right here in Broomstick is a brilliant wizard that can tutor her to bring out the best of her magical ability," said Mukul.

"He's here, in Broomstick? What's his name? Where can I find him?" asked Natee.

Howard was sitting there with an awkward expression with a quizzical look mixed in on his face. "And who did you say you were again?"

Mellissa field that question before Mukul could answer. "This wizard was a friend of my great grandmother, who happened to be a witch. He disguised himself as a handmade stuffed toy to get next to our daughter."

"That madam is not true. It was Shasta's idea that I watch over little Natee and protect her from the family if any of you discovered early in her life that she was a witch. And this morning I was there when she was poisoned by your prejudiced act of voodoo," explained Mukul.

"Uh, I'm not exactly following all of this. You're a wizard that was a friend of Natalie's great, great grandmother? That would make your age..." Howard was interrupted from two directions.

"It's Natee," said Natee.

"A few centuries to say the least," said Mukul.

"...and you are saying that because of the stuff that Melissa did with the brooms and the bay leaves poisoned Natalie because she is a..." again Howard was interrupted from two directions.

"It's Natee," said Natee.

"Don't say that word Howard, It's only helps his mind game against you," said Melissa.

"...a witch by passed down family traits, which for some unusual circumstances skipped two full generations," finished Mukul. "Or your wife would have been..."

"Now don't you say that about me! I won't befall to your macabre ways," said Melissa.

Howard stood up from the chair and said, "I need proof of what you're saying is true."

"Dad, I can see things. I can go places without leaving this house. That was how I knew how to get to where the bakery was." Natee sat down on the couch and closed her eyes. In a few seconds her face was paler and she looked cold to the touch.

"The bakery is completely burnt to the ground and there is a procession of mourners walking by leaving flowers for Winston Wisestone. Harriet is standing there with her head hung down with her fist clenched crying. Her sister is next to her trying to get her to come home. Down the line is a man wearing a black hooded robe with sandals carrying a wreath with lilies. If you leave now, you will see him placing the wreath on the site," said Natee as her face color came back.

Howard said, "It's not far from here. We could go and see what she said is true."

"You don't believe..." said Melissa. "Alright let's go." She pointed at Natee, "You had better be here when we get back."

"Excuse me but I must look into another matter," said Mukul with a very concerned expression on his face.

Natee sat there on the couch not moving. Her face color once again was fading. Howard and Melissa walked out of the house and got in their vehicle and drove down to the main road. Mukul stared for a moment at Natee before he faded away with a whisper.

Howard and Melissa slowly drove up to where they saw the long line of mourners. They were still blocks away from where the bakery was. They parked their car and started walking up the street looking at the strangely dressed people carrying flowers.

At the shopping mall they saw a black robed man just about to set a wreath with lilies. Melissa saw Natalie standing on the corner watching them. She walked over to her and was about to tell her "I told you to stay home." But Natalie wasn't really there. Melissa stepped back and tripped on Howard's shoes as he caught her.

The man in the black robe walked by the Keystone's not seeing the illumination of Natee. Howard and Melissa walked back to their car passing the people that were still in line to drop flowers.

"How could we have seen her and she not be there? How could she see the man in the black robe..." Howard's words trailed off.

When they got back to the ranch house Natee was sitting on the couch with a parchment paper in her hands. Her face was somber as their eyes met.

"I need both of you to sign this permission form for my tutoring."

"I'm still not signing anything that has to do with you becoming a witch. We bred that nonsense out of us long ago," said Melissa. "I don't want it to come back with all that strange freakish behavior and weird objects. No! I'm putting my foot down. Not here, not ever!"

"You knew this was going to happen. You knew Natalie had magical powers all along. It isn't what you have been saying all this time, trickery and mind games," said Howard staring at his wife.

Behind all of them Mukul appeared with a box. "Don't you think it is time to show Natee what you have hidden away all this time?"

Melissa looked at the old box with a grimace expression on her face.

Mukul said while holding the box, "Your mother has had the box since Shasta passed away,"

He opened the box to reveal its contents. There was an old hand bound leather book, a magic wand, two candle holders in the shape of women casting spells, and a large pumpkin size cauldron. Inside the cauldron was a hooded cape that smelled of old burnt incense.

"It didn't work. None of those spells or potions in that shadow book worked for me. I tried and tried to get that magic to do something. That's when I realized it was all rubbish," said Melissa. "Never, never again would I allow that…that hoodoo practice to enter my house again."

Natee was thumbing through Shasta's shadow book. "Wow, these are great spells. I can't wait to try some of them."

Melissa grabbed the book. "No. Didn't you hear me? I said no, never again in my house."

Natee ignored her mother and pulled out the hooded cape from the cauldron. Mysteriously from inside the cape an envelope fell to the floor. Written on it was 'To Natee'.

Natee bent over and picked it up. After a short examination she carefully peeled open the flap. Inside was a single folded sheet of writing paper.

Natee pulled out the paper and unfolded it. "It's a letter from Grandma Shasta."

> Dear Natee,
>   I wish I could have been there when you discovered your magical ability. Oh what a joy that would have been. But that was not to be, and I have gone on to Nirvana. Please help Mukul in removing the curse that plagues him. I could not, but I believe you can. I felt your magic, you can do it. Be a good

witch. Be a smart witch. Most of all, be a generous witch by giving to others.

Natee paused for just a second. "If any of the family stands in your way from doing this, hold my wand straight at them and say, 'Rattlesnake Salt'."

With Love,

Grandma Shasta

Natee quickly grabbed the magic wand from the box. Mukul tried to retrieve it from her.

"Not this time old man," said Natee as she pointed it at him. "Mom, Dad, please sign the paper. Grandma Shasta wouldn't have given me this spell if she didn't think it was necessary."

Both Howard and Melissa followed Natee over to the table where she sat down the parchment and the quill that Mukul had given her earlier. Howard picked up the quill and signed next to his name. The quill pricked the end of his finger and blood ran down to the point.

Melissa stared at Natee as she picked up the quill. After she had finished signing it was then both her and Howard noticed that they had signed in blood.

"Well you got what you wanted. Be a witch. But don't expect me to like it," said Melissa.

Natee brought Shasta's magic wand down to her side. "I'm sorry, that part about pointing the magic wand and saying rattlesnake salt, wasn't in the letter. I made it up. I saw the word in the shadow book. Trickery isn't magic. I should have said please."

Chapter Eleven
The Invisible Man
with the Fisheye

As the parchment paper and the quill faded away, Natee held Shasta's magic wand in her hands turning it over and over. It had an odd shape to it, rounded at the tip flattened as it curved in the middle, then back to being round and smooth to the end like a letter opener handle. "Will this be my magic wand?" asked Natee.

"All of this is yours," said Mukul.

"Don't let me see any of it scattered around the house, or out it goes with the trash," said Melissa.

Mukul on the other hand said, "You're not ready to use a magic wand. Just put the wand and the shadow book back in the box."

"Can I at least keep the cape?" asked Natee.

"Yes, you can keep the cape," said Mukul.

"Wash it first, that odor is obnoxious," said Melissa.

Mukul picked up the box with Shasta's things minus the cape and stepped back from the group "I will depart your presence as I have some important business to attend to. Natee, your things are in your room. Tonight, midnight and don't be late," said Mukul.

With a lifting of his staff, Mukul flashed from sight with a triumphant victory."

"What's at midnight?" Melissa asked.

"Witchcraft school," said Natee with happiness in her voice.

Natee went into her room. She was gleaming with excitement as she set up her things for witchcraft school. Natee then felt an urge that she needed to be somewhere else.

Natee felt dizzy. She drooped down on her bed. "I'm...I'm, coming. Who are you?"

Natee followed a man that was walking with a large five gallon glass bottle. The man had server burns to his upper body.

"Can I help you?" asked Natee.

"Magical medical ward...need Harriet."

Natee saw the emergency staff quickly took the man to the magical burn unit area. Natee stayed with the man all night.

Natee woke up the next morning knowing only that she needed to get Harriet Wisestone to the magical medical ward.

Without knowing how to use magic to get anywhere Natee walked down the main road to where there was a bus stop and waited. Coming down the road, Natee observed with curiosity, was a whirling dust cloud. It swooped her up like grabbing a house going to a magical land.

The next moment she was being kissed. "Hi Natee," said Wesley. "Mom told me about what happened yesterday morning."

"Oh it was an awful feeling. Things are better now. I have a lot to tell you, but I need to get to the Hidden Quiddity Potion Shop. Can you take me there?" asked Natee.

The swirling dust cloud stopped and Wesley said, "Something happened and I'm not supposed to go there right now. Even cousin Kizee isn't allowed. She is staying at a knotem's family's house."

"Your mom didn't tell you? Everyone is saying Winston Wisestone was killed by that monster that was haunting that strip mall. But Harriet is needed at the magical medical ward. There is a man there with half of his body burned. That is why I need to get to the potion shop. I must talk to Harriet," said Natee.

"If you promise not to tell my mom, I'll take you," said Wesley.

Natee said, "I read something that assures that I am telling the truth. It had something to do with crossing my fingers."

"I know that one. But if you break it bad things happen to you. It is cross my fingers and not to spell, and then you say what you are promising," explained Wesley.

Natee put up her right hand and crossed her fingers. "Cross my fingers and not to spell, I will not tell your mother that you took me to the Hidden Quiddity Potion Shop." Then Natee kissed Wesley to seal the promise.

Wesley held out his hand and Natee grabbed hold of it tightly. She knew this was going to be a rough ride.

Natee didn't get as sick as the first time. "Thank you Wesley," said Natee as she merged into the moving crowd.

Wesley yelled out, "I'll wait here for you." But he didn't think she heard him.

Natee moved through the crowd of people that were at the potion shop. Everyone was waiting their turn to give their condolences. It was late in the evening before Natee got close to

Harriet. "Harriet, Harriet I need to talk to you. It's important. Please let me through. Harriet, please I must tell you something important."

It was Agnes that heard Natee's desperate call. She motioned to some of the people to let Natee through to her. "What is it Natalie," asked Agnes.

"There is someone in the magical hospital that needs help," said Natee.

"They have a capable witchdoctor there. I'm sure they are receiving the best care they can offer," said Agnes.

"No...you don't understand, he needs help with another problem and I feel him calling out to Harriet about it," said Natee.

"I'm sure it can wait until they are better and can leave the hospital to see her. Harriet isn't in any mood to just leave right now," explained Agnes.

"But... But..." Natee was at a loss of words. The crowd pushed her back outside onto the sidewalk in front of the Moonlite and Spiders Crossquarter Festival glow-in-the-dark supply store. Wesley was waiting right there for her.

"You waited all the time for me? What if your mom finds out that you were here?" asked Natee.

"I don't care if she finds out. I wasn't going to leave you here. You're my friend, Natee." Wesley kicked the toe of his shoe at the sidewalk. "You're my only girl...friend. I mean, I wouldn't do this for my um, my cousin Kizee."

Natee looked at Wesley with a different point of view. She realized what she had said the first night to Wesley. *"You are the first person my age that I have met that can do real magic."* Wesley was her only friend, boy or girl.

"Wesley, thank you for being my friend," said Natee as she hugged him tightly. "You know I will take advantage of our friendship."

"I know, we're just friends and you'll dump me after you find out about him," said Wesley.

"Him? Him, who?" asked Natee.

"Him is the sixteen year old that all the girls want as their boyfriend. He rides in the jousting tournament at the Renaissance Faire. That is why I wanted you to meet me first," said Wesley.

Natee held up her hand and crossed her fingers. Wesley grabbed her hand. "No don't do that. Just promise me you'll stay my friend."

"I promise," said Natee. "I need to get to the magical hospital. Can you take me there?"

Wesley smiled and held out his hand and they vanished together.

Natee walked into the emergency room of the Broomstick hospital. She and Wesley walked up to the desk where a nurse was sitting. "An injured man came in early this morning."

"We get a lot of people through here, do you have a name?" asked the nurse.

"No, I haven't felt that yet, he doesn't know his name," said Natee. She tried to concentrate. It wasn't that easy for her to do. She was still feeling her way around with that magical ability. "He is in your magical medical ward."

"This is no place for practical jokes young lady. Now just leave before I call security," said the nurse.

As Natee and Wesley were walking away from the desk a doctor motioned to them. In a whisper he said, "Can I help you with something?"

Natee looked at the doctor and wondered why he was whispering. She whispered back, "An injured man came in early this morning who doesn't know who he is and no one can identify him."

"And you think you know who he is?" asked the doctor.

"Not yet, I need to get next to him before my magical power can help me do that," said Natee.

"Your magical power," said the doctor as he looked at the twelve year old girl and a boy about the same age. "Follow me."

The doctor brought Natee and Wesley to a corridor that had no doors or exit. "Down there you will find what you are looking for." The doctor scanned around to ensure no one had seen them. "Go, go quickly."

Natee and Wesley walked down the hall that went nowhere. The area turned dark like they were in an amusement park haunted house with no floor to speak of.

The area illuminated as Natee and Wesley walked. At the end was a desk with a nurse sitting there in a pure white robe and pointed hat.

"Can I help you?" said the nurse.

"An injured man came in this morning. I think I can identify him," said Natee.

"Is he a relative of yours?" asked the nurse.

Natee thought for a quick second. "He may be my uncle. He's my guardian."

"And what about you," asked the nurse to Wesley.

"I'm…her…um, cousin," said Wesley.

Natee and Wesley were escorted into the magical medical ward and over to a man that was bandaged from his head to his waist like the invisible man. Next to him sitting on a table was a large sealed glass bottle of water. Something was floating in the middle. Natee couldn't make out what it was.

Natee turned her attention to the bandaged man. In his ear she whispered, "I think I know who you are now. You're Winston Wisestone aren't you?"

Through the slits of the bandages Natee saw his eyes blink a couple of times then peered to move to match Natee's eyes.

"Nurse, this is Winston Wisestone," said Natee.

The nurse gestured to the witchdoctor. "This girl claims that this man is Winston Wisestone."

"That can't be true, he died in a fire last night," said the witchdoctor.

Natee said, "Just look into his eyes."

The witchdoctor pulled out his fisheye globe and stared into one of the man's eyes. Through the fisheye he saw in the man's eye an image of Harriet. "Get Franklin McDermit quickly and quietly."

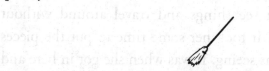

Agnes had finally managed to get everyone out of the potion shop and closed the door. Harriet was in shambles. She hadn't had any sleep since the news of Winston's tragedy, and she was still crying.

Agnes put Harriet to bed in her old room at the potion shop and she also went in the other room that had a bed. It was barely a couple of hours that she had fallen to sleep when a light tapping on the door to the room woke her up.

Agnes opened her eyes to see a shadowy figure was standing in the doorway. "Agnes," Franklin whispered. "Are you awake?"

"Franklin?" Yes, yes I'm awake," Agnes said softly.

"We need to go somewhere to talk alone," whispered Franklin.

Agnes got up and put on a hooded robe that she had at the shop for ceremonial spells and business related activities. Franklin held Agnes' hands and they faded out without making any noise.

"What are we doing here?" Agnes asked while standing in the magical medical ward.

"Do you see that girl over there next to the bandaged man?" asked Franklin.

"Yes, that is Natalie Keystone. Her family is staying at the Olsen's ranch house,"

"She is the girl that I have been tutoring," said Franklin.

"That girl is Natee? What is Mukul up to being covert with her and you?" asked Agnes.

"Her magical ability is limited, but she can do something extraordinary. She can see things and travel around without leaving where she is at. It took her some time to put the pieces together of what she was seeing. It was when she got in here and looked into that man's eyes that the whole story came to her."

"Natalie was at the potion shop last night trying to tell Harriet something. What is this all about?" inquired Agnes.

"The man came to the magical ward early this morning just after sunrise with magical burns on his arms and face carrying that glass bottle full of dingy water. Brace yourself, Agnes." Franklin paused before he said to Agnes, "Its Winston."

Agnes felt all her emotions rush through her like a bullet train through a tunnel. She collapsed into Franklin's arms.

She was revived with a smelling potion that also helped her get some energy. She sat up from the bed that was next to Winston's. "Why didn't they contact us earlier in the day?" asked Agnes.

"They didn't know who he was and he couldn't tell them either," answered Franklin.

"Mr. Franklin Sir?" said Natee.

"Yes Natee, what can I do for you?" asked Franklin.

"I'm going to miss school tonight," said Natee.

"Well I think what we will do is have a field trip. I think it is important for you to see the magical world that you are entering," said Franklin. "So pay attention, and you too Wesley."

"How are we going to tell Harriet?" asked Agnes.

"How about, 'when were you going to tell Harriet'," said Harriet as she walked into the medical ward.

"You should know by now, no one can keep secrets in this town. Right after you left a crowd of friends were banging on the potions shop door telling me Winston was here."

Harriet then dropped into a chair next to Winston's bed. Her crying started all over again, and the only thing she could think of saying to him was "Hiya, Winston."

Chapter Twelve
Who is on your Dark Side

Harriet stayed next to Winston for the next couple of days as the magical burn ointment and skin replicating bandages slowly began to heal him.

"It will take a few weeks for Mr. Wisestone to recover," said the witchdoctor.

"This was some serious magic he encountered. I've only read of this kind of magical burn happening once before in London in eighteen eighty eight. It was a strange case you see that involved the London Police Department..."

Harriet toned out the witchdoctor as he rambled on for the next half hour. She kissed Winston on the cheek that was still covered with bandages and went back to the potion shop.

"I want to thank Natee for what she did," said Harriet to Agnes. "It could have been many weeks before the medical staff could have recognized him."

Mukul happened to be at the potion shop and thought this would be a great opportunity for Natee. He wanted to make a suggestion, but kept it to himself. "You look very exhausted lady

Harriet. I'll leave you to let you relax and get some needed sleep," said Mukul.

Natee was sitting with Wesley on his front porch looking at a spell to preserve spider webs. He even had a book with some inside to show her.

"Excuse me Mr. Candlewick. I don't mean to interrupt your fun, but could I just have a few moments of Natee's time. I assure you I am not here to steal her heart," chuckled Mukul.

Natee walked off the porch and down to where Mukul was standing. She walked next to him as he escorted her far enough away for a private conversation.

"Harriet would like to do you a favor to repay your kindness for sticking to your story even when the adults didn't want to listen. It wouldn't be proper of me to suggest something directly without conferring with you first," said Mukul.

Natee said, "I don't want any reward or favors. I did it because it was the right thing to do."

"Yes, yes of course, you are absolutely right. But when one's wants to give you a gift, my mother gave me some good advice. Swallow your pride, smile, take it, and say thank you."

"What are you suggesting?" asked Natee.

"If she asks you, tell her that you would like a witch's coven to unlock your dormant magical ability," said Mukul.

"A witch's coven, what is that?" asked Natee.

"Well you see that right there should be a good reason to ask for it. To see a witch's coven first hand is better than me telling you. After all I have never been to one being that I am a wizard," said Mukul.

Since Franklin knew who Natee was and Natee knew who Franklin was, there was no need for the midnight secret sessions. She attended the afternoon program that Franklin had set up many years ago to help magical families train their children. Natee was having more fun with other kids around her age including Wesley and his cousin Kizee.

Then one day a tall young man came to one of the afternoon sessions. He needed help with a spell to complete his apprenticeship. He was very wide in the shoulders and his arms were too big for his shirt sleeves.

All the other young witches giggled to themselves trying to act mature and get his attention. "That's him, the one I told you about that competed in the jousting tournaments," said Wesley.

"What's his name?' asked Natee.

"Edward," said Wesley with a scowl expression.

"Have you ever talked to him?" asked Natee.

"Well, no, not directly," answered Wesley.

"Come on then," said Natee. She grabbed his arm and walked over to where Edward was sitting with a spell book.

"Hello Edward, my name is Natee and this is my boyfriend Wesley. I haven't seen you at the tournaments yet, but Wesley has. He says you're very good at jousting."

Edward sat there looking at them at first. "Hello Natee, Wesley.

That is kind of you to say that about my jousting." Edward was feeling just as awkward as Wesley was.

"Okay, that is not really why we came over here. Wesley was worried that once I met you that I would prefer you over him being that you are older and muscular and try to make you my boyfriend. Now isn't that silly," said Natee.

"Well I, that is, I already have a girlfriend, and um you are pretty, but I um, don't want to hurt your feelings. You aren't old enough for me," said Edward. "I need to study this spell. Maybe I'll see the two of you at the faire." Edward went back to reading his spell book.

After they walked away Wesley asked, "Did you really mean what you said back there? That I'm your boyfriend?"

"Yes, Wesley, I meant it. That is why I took you over there in the first place. Now stop worrying that I am going to dump you. It's you that will most likely dump me after you really get to know me," said Natee.

After the class was over Natee went over to the potion shop while Wesley had to go home for dinner. She was carrying a bag with Shasta's hooded cape in it. When she opened the door of the potion shop, Harriet rushed around the counter and gave Natee a big squeeze.

"I want to thank you for, for…" Harriet broke down and went back to crying.

Agnes freed Natee from Harriet and said, "Harriet is very grateful that you used your magical ability and found Winston alive."

"I came in to see if you could tell me how to clean my great, great grandmother's hooded cape. It was stuffed inside her cauldron for a few years," said Natee.

Agnes held up the cape and shook it out. "It does need that burnt smell removed. But it shouldn't be cleaned like any other garment would. This cape has magical spells embedded in its fabric."

Agnes took Natee into the back of the potion shop. "Have a seat. How did you come to be in possession of this cape?"

"Mukul brought a box that my mother had hidden away after my great, great grandmother had died. Inside were her shadow book, magic wand, candle holders, and a cauldron. This was stuffed inside the cauldron," said Natee.

"Where are the other things now?" asked Agnes.

"Mukul made me put them back in the box except her cape," answered Natee.

"Did you see her amulet in the box?" asked Agnes being suspicious of possible foul play.

"Mukul told me he has Shasta's magical amulet for safe keeping until he thinks I am ready to receive it," said Natee. "He told me something that I feel a little ashamed of knowing. He said that Harriet wanted to give me something for finding Mr. Wisestone. I don't deserve anything, so I don't want anything. But Mukul said I should ask Harriet to convene a witch's coven to unlock the rest of my magical ability."

Harriet, standing there looked at Natee then over to Agnes. "Unlock your magical ability? Who locked it up?"

Agnes stared into Natee's eyes deeply. Without a word she motioned her over to the large scrying mirror hanging on the wall.

"Look deep into the mirror with your arms stretched out in front of you. Now cross your left hand's first and second fingers," said Agnes.

In the mirror stood an image of Shasta with someone else smudged in the background. "Is that your grandmother?" asked Agnes.

"That is my great, great grandmother Shasta," said Natee.

Agnes stood there for a time. "Where is your great grandmother, and grandmother?"

"Mukul said that the family magic skipped two generations plus my two brothers," answered Natee.

"More like three and a half of generations. Switch crossed fingers to your other hand," said Agnes.

In the mirror with an extremely strong image was Shasta. She was wearing the hooded cape. Behind her was the same smudged image. Only this time Agnes could see who it was. She looked at Natee with a ponderous expression.

"What does all this mean?" asked Natee.

"You can put your arms down," said Agnes. "I um, I can clean the cape for you. It will take a few days." Agnes was pale and needed to sit down.

Harriet didn't see exactly what Agnes saw in the mirror so she asked. "What did you see in the mirror that made you look like you seen a ghost?"

"I ah, need to talk to someone else before I can answer that. Natee, do me a great favor. Don't tell anyone about what we saw in the scrying mirror, not even Wesley," said Agnes.

After Harriet took Natee home, she came right back and asked Agnes again, "What was that business with her great, great grandmother showing up like that on the black magic side? And what kind of magical spells are in this cape?"

"Harriet, Shasta was no ordinary witch. This cape is enchanted with protection spells," answered Agnes.

"How does this make Shasta special?" queried Harriet.

"The wearer of this cape can walk into the deepest corner of the Underworld unscathed if they wanted to," exclaimed Agnes.

Harriet's eyes widened with awe. "I would be very hesitant to try it. Do you think Shasta did just that?"

"I don't know. I do know this, Mukul is up to something that may cause a rift in the fabric of magic," said Agnes.

"What about Natee's magic being locked up and needing a witch's coven to unlock it?" asked Harriet.

"They are not locked up. Natee has her own amulet, just not mature yet. Mukul has Shasta's amulet and I bet he wants to keep it," said Agnes.

"Why do you suppose Mukul wants us to do a witches coven then?" asked Harriet.

"First I have to find out what he is up to. For now let's grant her, Mukul's wish. We'll convene a witch's coven that this town will never forget. To the Poison Apple Tavern for a witch consultation!" exclaimed Agnes.

"A witch's coven, you say. The likes no one has ever seen, you want. Dark and mysterious, you request. It shall be done," said Bee. She stood back from the table. "Did you like the theatrics?"

"That is exactly what I want," said Harriet.

Agnes usually doesn't go along with Harriet's pranks, but this sounded like a real good one. The witches giggled like young girls.

"It has to be in the forest where others can hide in the darkness behind trees. We need the most trusted friends that can keep this a secret until the very last minute," said Harriet.

They split up the details that each one was to carry out. To seal their secret fate the three witches held up their ale mugs and clang them together, "To the coven."

Chapter Thirteen
Nightmares and Daydreams

Natee was dropped off at her front porch by Harriet who then whisked away in the dark. "I can't wait till I can do that," said Natee.

It was late and Natee had been gone for almost another full day before showing up at the ranch house. She knew as soon as she opened the door trouble was waiting on the other side from her mother. She dreaded coming home.

It was dark in the house. Not a single bit of noise except the old grandfather clock's tick tock. She felt her way to her room and quietly closed the door before she turned on a light. Things were getting crazy for her.

"What was all that crossing fingers mumbo jumbo in front of that strange shiny black mirror?"

It didn't take Natee long to fall asleep after her head hit the pillow. Then the nightmare came. Shasta was wearing her hooded cape. Her face would be almost up against Natee's saying something that she couldn't understand. It seemed like a warning. From out of the cauldron, Natee observed, sooty steel blue smoke bellowing out with the stale smell of incense. Hideous creatures were crawling out, with fangs and sharp nailed claws. Their eyes were completely white except for the blood veins. The monsters were trying to grab her.

The Grendels had flesh falling off of their muscled skeleton figures. As they approached, burning acid drooled from their mouths. They were trying to surround Natee, wanting to eat her. Flying above her waiting their turn for scavenging were the Harpies. Their coarse feathered wings blending right into their skeletal arms. They would swoop down and screech from their gaping mouths filled with sharp pointed teeth and forked tongues.

Natee was running trying to fly to get away from all these monsters that were close behind her. She could smell their rotten raw meat hot breath and feel the needle point of their claws in her back. She woke up screaming into her pillow. Natee had spent the rest of the night in and out of sleep not wanting to have any reoccurring dreams.

Wesley was tapping on Natee's window early in the morning. Still dressed in her clothes from the day before, she got up and opened the window. "Agnes sent me to get you. She needs to talk to you about the witch's coven."

"Give me some time, I have to take a shower and change into clean clothes. I'll meet you out front in a half hour," said Natee. Then she closed the window and the curtain.

Wesley was on the front porch when Natee came out. He held out his hand, but before she took a hold of it she gave him a hug and a kiss.

"What was that for?" asked Wesley.

"I just hope someday you'll understand, when I go mad from the horrors that haunt me, I still want you as my boyfriend," said Natee.

She grabbed his hand and they were gone in a flash. Agnes was waiting at the potion shop for the two of them to arrive. "I had Wesley get you early because I want to ask you a lot of questions. I have a friend I want you to meet. Let me buy you breakfast."

Agnes led the way down the street to the Poison Apple Tavern not saying a word. Natee held Wesley's hand while they walked behind Agnes.

Natee looked at the double wood doors and the flaming sign just above them. "I didn't see this place in the virtual tour I did of Broomstick," said Natee.

The tavern was almost empty except for the Tavern Keep, Bee the waitress and a man sitting at a round table in the center of the tavern. Agnes offered Natee a seat next to the man sitting at the round table. Agnes took the only other chair next to Natee. Wesley sat on the other side of the round table across from Natee.

"Natee, this is James Candlewick. He is here to help us with granting your request for a witch's coven," said Agnes.

"Good morning Natee. Good morning Wesley. Let's break the cold chill here of you being surrounded by old adults. I'm here to find out how to unlock your magic. It will be a fun adventure, like going to a magic kingdom. Would you like that?" asked James with a smile.

Natee was apprehensive in saying something. He was the scariest wizard she had ever seen. He wore a heavy black robe with a hood that sat around his shoulders and neck. She was sure the hat that was hanging on the hat rack was his. It had a rolled brim with a cone shape that had stars and a crescent moon on it. He stared at her with piercing eyes like he was trying to read her mind.

"Well then, let's start with breakfast, shall we?" said James.

That was the signal for Bee and the Tavern Keep to come over to the table. They were carrying plates of blue scrambled eggs, some sort of sausage that might have been over cooked by the looks of it, and fruit that didn't fit any names that Natee knew. Appeared in front of her was some sort of pinkish cream in a crystal glass.

James kept the conversation light and made sure when he asked Natee a question she was in between bites and not chewing or swallowing her food.

"Tell me what you remember about your great, great grandmother," asked James.

While Natee picked at her food she told him of how Shasta was so happy to see her while the rest of the family stood back. "Grandma Shasta was always so nice to me. She would tell me stories that didn't make any sense though. I really can't remember any of them."

James made some notes as Natee talked, "Early childhood training."

Natee took a sip of the pinkish liquid and found it was sweet like a peppermint patty and tart like sugarless candy. It changed each time she took a sip.

"I do remember when she gave me the handmade stuffed toy black cat. She made me promise to keep it close to me at all times, and to never allow anyone to take him away. He would protect me. That was the last time I had seen her. There wasn't any kind of funeral. The family had her cremated," said Natee.

Natee paused and took a sip of the pinkish liquid. "My mom said years later something about the family attended a witch burning. I didn't understand until recently what was meant by that."

"What is that pouch that you have around your neck?" asked James.

"Mukul gave it to me just before he told me that I was to become a witch. It is to protect me from my family from ever harming me again," said Natee.

"Your family has harmed you in the past?" asked James.

"Just my brothers, they would hit me, pull pranks, and tell lies to get me into trouble," explained Natee. "After he gave me this, Donavan tried to grab me and burnt his fingers like he stuck them in a fire."

"Can I see that for a moment?" asked James.

Natee hesitated in removing it from around her neck.

"There is no one here that will harm you, I assure you," said James. He opened it and took a smidgen from the pouch. "Nail clippings, hair, dried skin and blood, from your family no doubt." He put the smidgen back into the pouch and handed it back to Natee.

During this whole time, James would look deeply into Natee's eyes while she talked. Finally Natee pulled out the letter from her great, great, grandmother's hooded cape and showed it to Agnes and James. "It fell out of the cape when I pulled it out of the cauldron."

"One last question Natee then I'll stop," said James. "When do you turn thirteen?"

"In two weeks, just before our vacation ends. But I won't have a party. I never had a party. I would spend my birthdays in my room in trouble for something that I didn't do," said Natee.

James wrote down, "Leo, the attribute of the lion is strength and fire."

Agnes moved a little closer to Natee. "This will be your best birthday ever. We are going to throw you a fantastic birthday party."

As they were finishing breakfast, James stared at Natee. His stare was hard and dense as if he was trying to penetrate lead with a laser pointer.

Back at the Hidden Quiddity Potion Shop Agnes asked Natee, "Would you like to help Wesley with the faire booth today? My daughter Wendy will be there. You'll enjoy meeting her."

Wesley smiled and said, "I'll show you some of the neat stuff we sell."

Once they were away, Harriet asked, "So how did breakfast go?"

"James said the only reason he could come up with why the magic skipped the three and a half generations and showed up in Natalie was because someone interfered. Her magic is practically all black." said Agnes. "Natee is more of a sorceress than a witch."

"Manipulated until ready by Mukul?" asked Harriet.

"We don't know how Mukul was able to do this yet," said Agnes. "James can't see into Natee. She has an impenetrable veil protecting her."

Harriet said to Agnes, "It's not a witch's coven she needs. It's a trial by fire. She is dangerous. We should just light her up and roast marshmallows for her birthday."

"Don't do anything until I get back from talking to Mukul. Do you understand? I don't want to come back to see you have set up a witch burning as a main event at the Renaissance Faire," said Agnes.

Natee was a little sleepy after breakfast and because she didn't get a good night's sleep. She was drowsy. Natee sat back in a chair in the corner of the potion booth and fell asleep.

She watched as a third person in her dream. *The organ played as dancers entered the jousting arena carrying torches of fire. Queen Elizabeth the first was in attendance to watch the afternoon event with Harriet sitting next to her feverishly laughing in that dream like fashion with echoes. In the middle of the arena was a huge stack of wood. It was surrounding someone tied to a center post.*

The dancers were well choreographed as they danced around the pile of wood in rhythm to the organ music. When the organ stopped playing, they all placed their torches to the wood. The blaze took off with a fiery roar. The crowd cheered as the blaze engulfed the whole scene. Natee changed from third person to the one tied to the post, screaming as she burned to death.

Natee woke up screaming with horrific pitch and volume. She was drenched from head to toe in sweat. "I-I got to go home," said Natee as she stared out at the jousting arena in the distance. "Tell Harriet I'm sorry to disappoint her, but I won't be attending her special event."

"There are a few things we need for the witch's coven," said Agnes as she sat in Mukul's one room shack trying to stay warm. "Natee will need Shasta's magical amulet and her wand. We will present them to her within the witch's circle under a controlled environment. Shasta's shadow book will be the key to release her power."

"How is the shadow book the key to releasing her magic?" asked Mukul knowing the real truth.

"I'm sorry I can't divulge that information. It is within the witch's circle that it can only be discussed," lied Agnes knowing full well that Mukul wasn't believing any of it.

"The amulet is too powerful to give to Natee right now. I promised Shasta that I would give it to her at the proper time. The magic wand must be kept safe also, until she has finished her training as a witch. Natee still has too much immaturity to be trusted with a magical instrument like a wand. She has threatened her family with it already."

"I'm not sure then we can help with a witch's coven then. All we can do is just give her our blessing on her thirteenth birthday," said Agnes.

"Her thirteenth birthday, I forgot it is coming up. Well yes, yes of course on her thirteenth birthday she should receive these things. I ah have a few things to attend to before I can give these items over to you. A few more promises I must keep prior to Natee receiving them," said Mukul a little feverishly.

"How is it that you became the keeper of Shasta's amulet instead of it going to her daughter?" asked Agnes.

"You ask a very good question, Agnes. And I really don't have the time to give you a good answer, except that I was her only friend at the time when she went on to Nirvana," said Mukul.

That was what Agnes wanted to hear. Her suspicions were confirmed of what she saw in the scrying mirror. Shasta's family held a private crematorium for their last witch in the family. If someone was looking they would have found that the magical amulet wasn't in the ashes.

"May I see the amulet, I need to know what particular color magic spell I need to use to transfer it over to Natee, when the right time comes," said Agnes.

Mukul held out the end of his staff where the amulet was kept in the globe. Agnes studied it carefully with her eyes as she could not touch it.

Agnes thought, "The amulet is Shasta's white magic that had been removed many years before by someone skillful enough and old enough to know how. He has been using it like a surrogate host until the time comes to give it up."

Agnes had gotten most of what she had come for. She was getting so cold that she had forgotten about the referenced in the letter of what Natee can do for Mukul.

Chapter Fourteen
What time of Life is it?

The bottle with the dingy water still sat next to Winston as he healed. Anytime someone would go near it or try to move it Winston would let out a moan heard clear across the entire magical medical ward.

While Agnes was talking to Mukul, Harriet visited Winston. She would gently rub the magical burn ointment onto the skin bandages. "It won't be too much longer before you will be able to move your mouth and tell me what is so important about this bottle of dirty water."

Harriet would tell Winston everything that had been going on unaware that anyone else was listening. "...and then Agnes said that Natee was more of a sorceress than a witch. I just made a suggestion that maybe it would be better for everyone if we just..." Harriet stopped talking when she got to the word burn. She thought that was not a good subject right now.

Agnes sat down in the far booth in the corner of the Poison Apple Tavern with Franklin and James.

"You were right James. He pulled most of Shasta's white magic right out of her. He has been using that amulet as his own," said Agnes.

"What about the reference in the letter?" James asked.

"It was extremely chilling up there. I don't know how he can live up there and not freeze to death," said Agnes. "I forgot to ask. I needed to get back to a warmer climate."

"We'll just have to figure out for what purpose Mukul needs a young sorceress. One thing about her black magic being so strong is I can't see her future. It is like she is completely invisible, almost nonexistent you might say. That protection pouch also has me baffled as well," said James.

"You said it only had in it the waste particles of her family members. How would that protect her from them?" asked Franklin.

James concluded, "I think it is the other way around. That pouch is protecting them from her if she decides to use her magic on them. That story of her brother getting his fingers burnt. The pouch didn't do that to him. It stopped her from completely incinerating Donavan into a screaming charred cadaver."

"Why give her a protection pouch now and not before? I mean what has changed that would make her magic do things now that didn't happen while she was growing up," asked Agnes.

Her face turned from a questionable look to a concerned one instantly. "Oh! I just figured it all out. I'll see you two later," said Agnes.

Wendy was helping one of their regular customers when Agnes showed up at the Renaissance Faire booth. "Where are Natee and Wesley?"

Wendy told her mother of Natee waking up and screaming. "Wesley took her home a few hours ago."

Agnes left the renaissance fair and showed up at the ranch house. Agnes found Natee and Wesley swimming in the pool. She sent Wesley home.

Natee went and changed clothes while Agnes and Melissa sat down at the dining table. When Natee sat down at the table, Agnes pulled Shasta's cape from her bag and placed it on the table.

Natee quickly grabbed it before her mother had the chance of taking it away. She put it to her nose and smelled it. It had whispers of orange blossoms.

"You just started having these nightmares or illusions just before you came here to Broomstick. Did something else happen at the same time?"

"What are you getting at?" asked Melissa wondering why Agnes was prying into Natee's personal life.

"Melissa, she is twelve going on thirteen in a couple of weeks. This is very important," said Agnes.

"Alright, yes." said Natee. "I didn't want to tell anyone about the curse."

Melissa asked, "About what curse?"

"Melissa, you know, THE CURSE," answered Agnes with a tone of voice to accent the meaning.

"Tell us how your period started," requested Agnes.

"The first one was a month ago. It was more of a daydream of being shackled to the bed and having an exorcism as a punishment for being a witch. It was a mess. I cleaned up the blood and hid the sheets because you would have just punished me for something else I had no control over," said Natee.

"That's not true. I wouldn't have punished you," said Melissa.

"Now it time for your next one," said Agnes.

"It hasn't started yet, but it will be soon. The other night I had a nightmare with monsters wanting to eat my flesh. It was so real."

"And today, what was that one about that had you screaming," asked Agnes.

"Harriet arranged to have me burned at the stake for being a witch as a main attraction for the Queen," said Natee. "Am I going mad like they say just before it happens?"

"Melissa, sit here and talk to your daughter. I have a witch's coven to stop," said Agnes.

"Talk about what, her becoming a witch?" asked Melissa.

When Agnes got back to the Hidden Quiddity Potion Shop, Harriet was there waiting for her. "I don't know how it leaked out. I didn't tell anyone."

"Is this about the witch's coven?" asked Agnes.

"The whole town knows about Natee. There might be trouble," said Harriet.

"What are you talking about?" insisted Agnes.

"They heard that Natee is a sorceress," said Harriet.

"I leave for a few hours and somehow things manage to get completely fouled up. Who did you tell that Natee was a sorceress?" questioned Agnes.

"I didn't tell anyone. Right after you left I went to see Winston at the magical medical ward and I just got back from there the same time you showed up here," said Harriet.

"You told Winston, didn't you," said Agnes.

"Well yes I guess so, but he still can't talk yet," answered Harriet.

"No, he can't talk. How about other patients, their visitors and the medical staff? They have ears and can talk," said Agnes.

Agnes just stood there thinking what to do next. "Let's go. We have to save Natee from whomever," said Agnes.

The two of them appeared at the front door of the ranch house. All seemed quiet, no mob was there storming the place. Agnes knocked on the door. She was about to knock again when Howard opened the door.

"Hello, I'm Agnes and this is my sister Harriet. We need to talk to Natee and Melissa."

Melissa was coming up behind Howard saying, "Natee isn't here. Mukul and she had to go to meet her magic instructor or some sort of person like that."

"We're too late," said Agnes. "I should have seen this coming when I mentioned her thirteenth birthday was coming up and he got nervous about the time."

"Too late for what?" asked Melissa.

"To stop Mukul and whatever he has planned for Natee to do as a sorceress before her thirteenth birthday," said Agnes.

Mukul had Natee sit at the table in his one room shack. The potbelly stove was full with burning wood to make the place as warm as possible.

He was applying makeup to her face. Around her eyes and across the bridge of her nose he painted white with an outline of blue. Down her cheeks angling from just under her eyes to her jaw line were three stripes, white-blue-white. Her hair was tucked into a bun with the hair covering her ears.

He had her put on Shasta's hooded cape with special protection charm spells attached to the fabric. Under the cape Natee was wearing a black ruffled body suit with black boots up to her knees. Black silk gloves ran up her arms under the wide sleeves of the cape.

"At the entrance use the calling spell for the unicorn at the clear pool of water. Once she has appeared, gently sit on her back, lady like. She will take you into the realm. You are looking for a shattered amulet. Collect every piece of it, leave not a sliver behind. Do not touch any of the shards with your bare hands. Put it in this pouch. Now be careful and don't use the wand unless it is absolutely necessary. Remember principal number three while you are in there." commanded Mukul.

Mukul pointed the globe at the end of his staff at Natee. He mumbled some words that she could not understand as she was whisked away to the entrance of the Realm of Forbidden Magic.

When Agnes arrived Mukul was not at his shack on top of the mountain. She found makeup sitting on the table.

"Magical face paint," said Agnes.

Natee's clothes were lying on the old bed. Agnes was thinking the worst as in, "Mukul may be involved in some kind of black magic blood sacrifice of Natee. But to what end?"

Back at the Poison Apple Tavern, Agnes told of what she had found at Mukul's shack. James had some information that didn't calmed down Agnes' fears.

"Even in our magical world some information does get lost. But I have found that our friend has been through a witch's council. It's not clear of the exact charges other than he was involved in a revolt that may have had something to do with him killing a young girl. Have any of you seen the palm of his left hand?" asked James.

"If you are referring to the scar, I have seen it," said Franklin. "He said it was given to him at a rite of passage when he was much younger and a lot less wise than he should have been."

"Did it look like a spider?" asked James.

Franklin thought for a moment. "I'm not sure. With his hand partially closed some of the lines could have looked like wrinkles."

"It just might be the curse of the spider that he received instead of being executed. Our wizard has been around for quite a long time," said James.

"What is he doing with Natee then? He has manipulated the family to produce a girl with almost total black magic powers. He has taken her away somewhere painted up with magical paint just at the age that she is changing into a woman. I want to be the executioner at his next council," said Harriet.

"Harriet do you really feel that way about me?" asked Mukul as he walked into the Poison Apple Tavern.

"What have you done with Natee you monster?" yelled Harriet.

"Relax my dear, Natee is safe. She is just doing me a pure hearted favor. She will be back in time for your little witch's coven on her thirteenth birthday in which you will do what your circle does," said Mukul.

"That doesn't answer my Sister's question," said Agnes.

"If you must know she is in the Realm of Forbidden Magic. She is retrieving what was wrongly taken from me many years ago," said Mukul.

James with a calm voice said, "Don't you mean many centuries ago?"

"You figured it out I see," said Mukul. He held out his left hand and showed the scar in the palm that looked like a spider.

"You know, one of the things we wizards have always been striving for was immortality. This ironically isn't it. To live with barely enough magic to do simple tasks and to carry a soul of a little girl inside you screaming relentlessly for peace and understanding isn't any way to exist. And what of this curse, I am to wait until I am vanquished by a pure hearted act."

Mukul walked over to the bar. "Ale if you please." He slugged it down and slammed the mug down on the bar.

"I am not waiting any longer. Instead, I have made that pure hearted act come to me. Natee is going to get my amulet back for me. And there is nothing any of you can do to stop it."

Chapter Fifteen
The Realm of
Forbidden Magic

No one could enter the Realm of Forbidden Magic without first passing the three tests. The first test is to summon the unicorn. Only virgins could do this as they are the only ones that can see the unicorn.

Natee sat at the edge of the water. She gazed at her reflection. It was strange to her as she didn't see what she looked like after the makeup was applied. She said, "Beautifully adorned, never scorned, pure as light lovely Unicorn. Appear to me in my sight above me this morn."

Natee saw in the reflection a white horse with a horn extending from its forehead. Carefully she turned to look at the unicorn directly. Her mane was pure silver white that glistened in the sun.

The second test is riding on the back of the unicorn. Together they will enter the tunnel that leads to the Realm of Forbidden Magic.

Natee slowly and gracefully got up from the pool of water. Standing on the left side of the unicorn she moved the unicorn over to a nearby rock to allow her to sit down on its back. The unicorn began to move and Natee was off to the tunnel.

The third test is to transverse the tunnel. It is in the tunnel that Natee must be invisible inside and out.

Inside the tunnel, her black wardrobe, the mask and her black magic hid her from the Grendels that watched the tunnel from the walls. Hanging above her were the Harpies waiting for any sign of movement. Natee kept very quiet. The only sound was the echo of the unicorn's hoofs clopping on the floor of the tunnel.

At the end of the tunnel was the realm. It wasn't anything like Natee had imagined. She thought it would have blue skies and singing birds with lush trees. Instead the sky was gray and brown. The ground was just dirt with nothing growing. There were boulders scattered about like trash.

"What is this place?" asked Natee.

The unicorn stopped just after they had entered the realm. Natee slid off her back onto the crystalline sand. Before she could say wait, the unicorn trotted back to the tunnel and was gone.

"Where do I go from here?" said Natee aloud to no one.

Although there wasn't a clear path to anywhere, Natee did notice that the bigger boulders were scattered almost as guideposts. She walked from one to the other finding nothing not even a single shard of Mukul's amulet.

The trail of boulders ended at a flat rock table. Cut into it was a groove with a small bump in the middle, like something was to be inserted into it. Natee looked around, but all she saw were rocks of all sizes.

Then she saw a smooth rock that didn't look like the rest. It was slender with a segment missing from the center. Natee quickly picked it up and placed it in the groove.

A thunderous sound prevailed as the ground around her fell away with earthquake seismic waves shaking her to the ground. After it was over Natee saw that the land had opened up with a canyon that stretched to the horizon. There was a trail that led down into the canyon. Natee wished that she had that unicorn to ride on.

The trail was long and narrow along the face of the canyon. About half way down she could see the bottom of the canyon. A river flowed through it with white foam splashing off the rocks.

At the bottom Natee sat down by the edge of the river. She took off one of her gloves to retrieve some water for a drink.

"Who dare drink the water of the Realm of Forbidden Magic?"

Natee jumped back and pulled her glove back on. It was too late. She had let her presence be known.

A face made by the water stood in front of Natee. "You cannot hide yourself any longer. The realm knows why you are here."

"Then if you please, could you direct me to the amulet of Mukul and I'll just be on my way," said Natee.

"Do you not know why it is here?" said the water face.

"Yes, I know why it is here. It was unjustly taken away from him for an act that did not deserve punishment," said Natee.

"You must seek the forbidden knowledge behind the circumstances to see the truth. Go and find the pool at the end of the river. Call upon the fairy that lives there by throwing ten gold coins into the pool of water," said the water face. The water splashed back into the river leaving Natee alone once again.

"Gold coins, where am I going to get gold coins?" asked Natee.

From behind a boulder a gruff voice said, "You can sell something to get gold coins, like your black cape."

Natee turned around to see standing next to the boulder where the voice came from was a troll. His head was a rounded cube with hair and a beard that ran together. His eyebrows were one solid line across his forehead with small beady eyes underneath. He had a big nostril'ed nose with a wide mouth that stretched completely from one side of his face to the other.

"What are you?" asked Natee.

"I'm a type of troll," said the troll. "What are you?"

"I'm a witch, a very powerful witch I might add," said Natee.

"Well very powerful witch, why don't you just make gold coins rain down from the sky?" said the troll.

"That is against the principals of magic and nature," said Natee.

"Well then I guess you'll have to sell that cape to get your gold coins. I will give you ten gold coins for it. That is how much you'll need to talk to the fairy of the Pool of Forbidden Knowledge," said the troll.

Natee wasn't fooled by this troll. "This cape is very magical. It is worth five thousand gold coins."

"Oh, but do you see anyone here willing to give you that much? My offer stands, ten gold coins," said the troll.

"I don't think you are the only inhabitant of this realm. I will look for someone else to deal with, maybe even an enemy of yours. I bet they would pay me five thousand gold coins to eliminate you. I will keep my cape, gain five thousand gold coins, and use my magic to shrink you down to bug size and step on you," said Natee. She turned away from the troll and started walking off.

"Er wait, maybe I was a bit hasty with that offer. How about one hundred gold coins?" said the troll.

Natee looked over her shoulder at the troll. "Forty five hundred gold coins."

"Go, go and find someone else to deal with, the most you'll get is seven hundred gold coins," said the troll.

Natee kept walking as the troll followed behind her. "Instead of the cape I'll offer you one wish for all the gold in your bag."

The troll stopped and rubbed his scruffy beard knowing the bag is really empty. "How about two wishes?"

"Nope, just one wish," said Natee.

The troll squinted his beady eyes and shown his yellow stained teeth while sucking in air through them. Finally he said, "Alright, it's a deal. One wish for the bag."

The troll handed Natee the empty bag. Natee quickly noticed the bag felt empty. Knowing what the exact wording was of their deal, a wish for the bag, she didn't say anything about it.

"Now what is your wish?" asked Natee.

"Um, I ah, I wish for, hum?" said the troll.

"Come on hurry up I have things to do," said Natee as she tried to rush the troll into making a mistake.

"I wish for a, um, I wish for a…" mumbled the troll.

Natee heard the troll's stomach rumble which gave her a way out of this situation. She said, "Can you please make a decision. I'm getting hungry and I have a sandwich and cold drink going to waste."

The troll's eyes opened up wide, "I'm hungry too. I wish I had a sandwich."

Natee smiled at the troll. "You have made your wish." She took out the magic wand as to grant the wish. She really had it ready just in case the troll decided to lunge at her after she granted the wish. "You'll never starve again, for you can eat the sand which is here in this realm."

The troll stood there dumbfounded. "You tricked me. That wasn't my wish."

"You cheated me by trading an empty bag. That's makes us even," said Natee.

Natee started walking away to follow the river to find the pool of water with the fairy in it.

"Wait," said the troll. "The bag has magic powers to give the owner only what they need in gold, not what they want. When the time comes there will be your ten gold coins in the bag."

"When the time comes then I will give you the sandwich you wished for," answered Natee.

"Wait, I can help you. There are dangerous creatures out here."

"Okay then, I'll pay you one hundred gold coins to be my guide, and no haggling," said Natee.

The troll smiled and said, "It's a deal."

Natee reached into the bag and to her amazement she pulled out one hundred gold coins. She handed the troll his gold coins and asked, "Do you have a name?"

"Sebastian," said the troll.

"Okay Sebastian, my name is Natee. Lead the way to the pool at the end of the river."

Sebastian started down the trail bobbing from side to side as he walked. Natee kept the wand close at hand as she didn't trust her new friend or anything in this realm.

"Do you know where the smashed amulet of Mukul the wizard is kept?" asked Natee.

Sebastian talked over his shoulder, "I know nothing of any amulet here, smashed or otherwise."

Sebastian led Natee down a trail that followed the small river. At one point Sebastian stopped by the edge of the water and turned over a large rock. Under it was squiggly greenish brown creatures that were long and slimy with too many little legs to count.

"Here, you want one?" asked Sebastian as he held out one to Natee.

"No thanks, you can have all you want," said Natee not wanting to even look at them.

A voice came from behind some large boulders. "Hello, Sebastian. Who's your friend?"

With one of those icky creatures hanging out of his mouth, Sebastian turns around to face the voice.

Two trolls came out of hiding and walked close to Sebastian and Natee. "I asked you a question, Sebastian."

They looked about the same to Natee as Sebastian with some minor cosmetic differences. "She's a very powerful witch. I suggest you just leave us alone," said Sebastian.

"A witch? Here in the realm? There has never been a witch but one that could get passed the Grendels and the Harpies and live," said the first troll. "And she is long gone never to return."

"But I have returned," said Natee. "I got passed them with ease once again. I am surrounded with dark magic more powerful that this realm has to offer. Care to have me use my magic on you that I used on them?" She raised both of her gloved hands high above her head and pointed two finger of each hand at them.

The trolls looked more curious than frighten until Natee started to say something. "Rotten apple, poison dirt…"

That was enough for the two trolls. They scampered up and away from the water's edge back into the shadows of the boulders.

"Hey, you are a powerful witch. Nothing has ever scared them. What would you have done to them?" asked Sebastian.

"It would be better for you not to know and trust I don't do it to you," said Natee with little beads of sweat on her forehead. She relaxed a little, but was still worried if her fake spell hadn't worked what would she had done.

Natee didn't know Shasta's cape would have done anything spell fake or otherwise.

Darkness was taking over the sky and Natee was feeling scared. She hadn't eaten and was afraid to drink any more water from the river. Sebastian kept himself fed by eating those ugly creatures that live under the rocks by the water's edge.

Natee thought back to some of the spells that she had learned from witchcraft school that demonstrated the principles of magic. One had to do with cooking magic. So she found a flat rock and tried a spell with the wand.

She twirled the wand in a clockwise circle while concentrating on one thing only. "Cheese pizza."

Natee got just a little more than she was thinking about. Next to the pizza was a cup with something to drink. She picked up a slice of pizza and took a small bite. "Mumm," said Natee. Then she sipped some of the drink. It was a new strange flavor of carbonated soda she had never had before. One thing she noticed about it was that it was very foamy.

Before she finished eating, it had become completely dark. There weren't any stars or moon for light. It was like sitting inside the bedroom closet. Natee had done that many times as a little girl because of the torment that she received from her brothers. This was different. There weren't any walls around her to make her feel safe.

The sounds of the night were eerie. Natee thought she felt something crawling on her. She pulled out the magic wand and drew a circle around her to give the feeling of a wall, and then she held the wand with both hands. She was sitting with her knees touching her chin. She said, "Magic wand, protect me."

Natee awoke lying on her side still with her knees touching her chin and both hands holding the magic wand. When she opened her eyes, she found herself staring at the charred face of a Grendel.

Natee quickly scooted away and got to her feet. She was pointing the magic wand at the dead creature. Taking in air with deep breaths, being scared out of her wits, she jumped at a noise that came from her right side. She swung the wand over to that direction. Sebastian was turning over rocks to find the grub like creatures at the edge of the river.

When he saw Natee pointing the wand at him, he fell and splashed backward and away from her.

There were noises up in the rocks as well and she pointed the wand at that direction. The trolls looked at the scene of the dead Grendel and Natee pointing a magic wand at them. They dropped back behind the rocks.

Natee finally relaxed a little and brought the wand down in front of her. "Sebastian, tell your friends up there that I want something to eat, and not those things from under the rocks. I want fruit and something to drink other than the river water."

Within minutes there were trolls coming down from the rocks cautiously carrying a basket of fruit and a jug. They sat them down and backed off.

Natee examined the fruit and picked out something that resembled a banana. Then she picked up the jug and took a taste. It was sweet like guava juice.

Once Natee was satisfied with breakfast, she said to Sebastian, "Alright let's get on with it."

Down the trail they went.

At supper time, the trolls did the same thing of setting a basket of fruit and a jug for Natee then backing off. "Sebastian, tonight I want a fire, a large fire to be kept burning all night."

As the light faded away, the trolls piled up wood and lit it. Natee kept near the fire but also drew a circle around her again and held the wand in her hands as she went to sleep.

Natee was careful when she opened her eyes as she did not want to see another dead creature lying next to her.

The sky was lit up and blue. The night fire was now just smoking embers and a basket of fruit and a jug were waiting for her.

A few hours later Natee and Sebastian stood at the edge of the pool where the river water flowed in. It was deep and dark at the bottom. Natee counted out ten gold coins and tossed them into the pool of water.

The coins shimmered as they fell through the water. The water gently swirled with glistening little stars. Natee watched as someone came up from the water and floated in the air in front of her.

The fairy had long and wide wings like a Polynesian forest butterfly. She stared at Natee with huge wide ocean blue eyes.

Not knowing what to really do Natee bowed to the fairy and said, "If it isn't too much trouble, my question to you is, 'where can I find the shattered amulet of Mukul the wizard?"

The fairy spoke in a soothing voice. "Ignore the obvious, capitalize on the impervious. The path to the truth is not always clear, but true intentions show themselves at the last possible moment. Truth lies within the sound. That is where your lost soul will be found."

Before Natee could ask what all that meant the fairy had vanished back into the water. "You live here, what did that all mean to you?" Natee said to Sebastian.

He just rocked side to side with his eyes looking up as he shrugged his shoulders. Natee sat down on the edge of the pool and stared into the water from where the fairy had come out of. The water that was flowing into the pool was making a rushing sound as it fell and splashed.

"What other sounds have I heard in this realm?" asked Natee aloud. She got up and walked away from the pool shaking her head. "I've come all this way just to find a dead end with a nonsense statement from a fairy that lives in a pool of water at the end of a river."

Then Natee grabbed a large heavy rock, walked back over to the pool. Without saying a word she jumped in feet first clutching the rock tightly.

Chapter Sixteen
Not so Obvious

Natee held the rock tightly as she plunged deeper into the pool. Light was fading rapidly and she was beginning to think this may have not been a good idea after all. She was running out of air in her lungs.

Natee let go of the rock. But instead of the rock falling away downward it began to float up. She noticed the color change of the water below her was lighting up. She turned around and began to swim downward.

To her surprise and relief, her head popped up to the surface. Natee gasped for air and filled her lungs to capacity. She held it for a few seconds then let it out. She sucked in a second large breath of air and held it for another few seconds again.

Natee slowly let her breath out and began to breathe normal as she made her way to the edge of the pool. She looked for Sebastian, but he wasn't anywhere in sight.

"Wait, the water is flowing out of the pool. I was right," exclaimed Natee aloud. She sat on the edge of the pool and thought of what her next move should be.

"I don't have Sebastian as a guide anymore or the other trolls to fetch me food," said Natee aloud.

She was looking around for someone up in the rocks that might be watching her. No one was there.

Natee picked herself up and began to walk in the direction of where the water was going. As she emerged from the rocky seclusion where the pool was almost hidden, the landscape changed. It wasn't that sandy rock canyon anymore.

There were trees and shrubs with wild grass. Natee wasn't sure, but she thought she heard birds chirping. She kept to the edge of the river and did not let the pleasant surroundings fool her. She remembered the first part of what the fairy had said. "Ignore the obvious, capitalize on the impervious."

This was what made Natee grabbed the rock and jump into the pool. The obvious was that she would sink to the bottom. But the passage was there because the water flowed in and not out. Now being on the other side Natee was looking at the obvious.

"This is what I expected the realm to look like. Another definition for impervious is 'uninfluenceable', I must capitalize on this. I will not be influenced by what I see."

"Ignore the obvious, capitalize on the impervious. The path to the truth is not always clear, but true intentions show themselves at the last possible moment. Truth lies within the sound. That is where your lost soul will be found," repeated Natee.

"True intentions show themselves at the last possible moment." Natee pulled out the wand and started walking.

The light began to change and Natee knew that darkness was coming. She found a clearing and gathered up some fallen wood. With the wand she sparked a small flame. After the fire was going she used the wand to draw a circle around her and the fire. "I need a cauldron full of stew, a bowl and a spoon."

Natee concentrated while holding the wand with both hands and pointing at the ground. A small cauldron with some kind of liquid appeared with a bowl and spoon sitting next to it. She placed the cauldron next to the fire and waited for it to get warm.

While waiting, Natee held the wand up over her head and said "Magic wand protect me." Nothing really happened, but each night she had said that.

Natee put a few more twigs onto the fire as she sat there eating the warm stew. There were sounds around her that made her skin crawl. Snarls and gnashing of teeth came from all directions. She couldn't see what was making the electrical zapping noise above her, but she had a guess that something was flying and touching her protective magical dome that surrounded her.

"I don't think I'm going to get much sleep tonight," she said to herself.

Very late at night Natee was awaken by someone talking to her. The fire was just embers.

"Come on out and play, little girl," said the voice in the dark.

Natee replied while holding the wand tight, "Who's there?"

"Come on out and play with us," said the voice.

Natee sat up and placed some twigs on the embers and fanned them with her hand to get the fire started for light. A streak of sparks came around her with the sound of fingernails being pulled across a chalkboard.

"Come with me little girl on a magic journey," said the voice in the dark.

"What do you want? If it is trouble you're looking for then you found the right witch to mess with," said Natee trying to sound fearful.

"I can show you what you are looking for. I will take you to where it is hidden," said the voice again scratching its nails around her protective field.

Natee now had the upper hand in this game of wits. "You know where it is hidden and you can take me there?" said Natee. "I don't believe you. You have no idea where the magic lamp is with the most powerful genie is kept." Natee hoped the creature would take the bait.

"Oh but I do, I have seen it with my own eyes," said the voice. "I can take you there. All you have to do is step out of your circle and we will be off."

Natee set a couple of twigs on the fire and held the wand that much tighter. "I'm not going with you anywhere." Natee ignored the voice for the rest of the night. She didn't get any more sleep until the sky started to lighten up and the voices went away.

When she did awake, it was to a fully bright blue sky. She could see that the clearing outside of where she drew her circle was torn up and dirt was flung everywhere with heavy clawed marks all around.

Natee made the cauldron and eating utensils disappear and checked that the fire was completely out.

Holding the wand in front of her she stepped out of the circle and began following the river. The river began cutting down into the ground and following it was becoming difficult. It was too swift to float or swim. If Natee had a boat it would be smashed on the rocks.

She sat there on a large rock and looked down at the river. While she thought of her choices, she twirled the wand and made a cheese pizza appear with that unusual drink that came with it. As she sat and ate a slice, small animals were scurrying in all directions. Then she heard the stomping of a large beast. Before she could get up she felt hot air flowing on her. She slipped off the rock and fell onto the ground.

A creature the size of a baby elephant that looked like a prehistoric museum exhibit shuffled up to where Natee was. It had a horned head, a long tail and purple scaled skin. It scooted forward, but not at Natee. It moved toward the pizza.

It turned its head to Natee and puffed a couple of smoke rings with a whimper then turned back to the pizza.

"The pizza, you want the pizza?" said Natee.

Natee stood up and stepped further away from the rock where the pizza sat. "Go ahead it's all yours, purple pizza eater."

Again the creature turned its head toward Natee and puffed a couple of smoke rings with a whimper. Natee did a daring move. She stepped closer to the scaly monster and picked up a slice of the pizza. "Here you go, little dragon."

The dragon opened its mouth and waited for Natee to throw the pizza into it. She could see the large pointed fanged teeth that could just as well have chewed her up like a snack.

Natee picked up another piece and tossed it into its mouth. "Here's the last piece," as she threw it onto the dragon's tongue.

"Now you're going to eat me," said Natee.

The dragon shook its head and stared at her.

"You understood what I just said?" asked Natee. "Are you a wizard or some kind of enchanted person?"

The dragon shook its head no at Natee.

"You're a real true to life dragon then," said Natee.

The dragon nodded its head.

"Can you fly?" asked Natee.

The dragon held out its front claw with a bat like structured wing.

"You aren't going to eat me later or something. I mean I am getting the feeling you want to be my friend. The question is why do you want to be my friend? I've read stories that dragons breathe fire and eat virgins," said Natee.

The dragon puffed smoke rings and made gurgling sounds.

"You're laughing at me. You are laughing at me! I didn't write the stories. If they're not true then why would someone say that about someone as sweet as you?" said Natee.

The dragon closed its eyes and turned away for a moment.

"I'm sorry I didn't mean to embarrass you," said Natee.

"Since you can fly, could you take me to where the river ends?" asked Natee.

The dragon nodded and crouched down to let Natee crawl up on her back. She held onto the dragon's purple scales as tight as she could. Natee was scared, a different kind of scared then the night before, still she was scared.

The dragon stomped its way to the edge of the rocky cliff just above the river and dove off plunging down. Then the dragon opened it wings and caught some air.

Natee was screaming the whole time as she hung on for life. Once they were level and the dragon was gently flapping its wings, Natee decided to open her eyes.

There wasn't much of a view as the dragon's wings were in the way. The glimpses that she did see, was the land was leveling out and the canyon walls were tapering away. The trees were replaced by shrubs, plants and sand dunes.

The dragon started a decent. Natee didn't know what kind of landing a dragon does so she braced herself and tightened her grip to the dragon with her legs.

The dragon flapped it wings hard and hovered over a clearing. Natee felt the dragon's back legs touch the ground and bend to take the weight. The dragon tucked its wings in and put the front claws down on the ground.

Natee half slipped off with using the scales as steps. She looked around to find the river was over to her left. It was running into the ocean. Natee was standing on a beach. The waves were making a majestic sound. Off in the distance off shore was an island.

At first Natee thought she was at another dead end until she stared at the island. "Truth lies within the sound. That is where your lost soul will be found. This isn't an ocean. It's a sea or a bay. No, it's a sound. Truth lies within the sound!"

The sky was beginning to dim and Natee knew what that meant, another night of horror. "Let's get ready for darkness," said Natee.

She moved off the beach and up to a bluff. She gathered wood for a large and long burning fire. She made several pizzas for her dragon friend. While Natee fed it she asked it questions that the dragon could respond to.

"I don't suppose you have a name. And if you did you couldn't tell me what it was," said Natee. "Can I give you a name?"

The dragon nodded its head

"Hmm, are you a boy or a girl dragon?" asked Natee. "Well let's start with, are you a boy dragon?"

The dragon shook it head side to side.

"Okay then, a girl's name. How about Sara?" asked Natee.

The dragon nodded in agreement.

"Very well Sara, do you know about the terrible creatures that come out at night?" asked Natee.

Sara nodded and blew black smoke rings with a grunt.

"If I drew a magical circle in the dirt around me would you stay out and not disturb it?" asked Natee. She didn't want to take the chance of both of them in the circle and having her leave or move.

After about ten pizzas Natee said, "I think you had enough."

Sara nodded in agreement.

Natee went on to set up her fire and the magical circle. She conjured up the cauldron, bowl, and spoon. Then she held the wand up over her head and said, "Magic wand, protect me."

Natee's fire was going good and her stew was hot compared to the night before. Darkness came and the sounds of horror were once again all around her.

At first Sara was lying down nearby, but later she had slipped away quietly in the dark. Then the flashes of fire began with thunderous roars followed by the screaming of tortured creatures. Natee noticed that the darkness became quiet, and she fell to sleep.

Chapter Seventeen
The Island of Truth

The waves were crashing onto the shore with a roar that finished up with a sizzling sound of the water bubbling down into the sand. Natee woke feeling refreshed as she breathed in the salty air. Sara was lying not too far away curled up like an oversized stuffed toy, like the one you would win at a carnival.

When Natee stood up, she saw smoke coming from the distant island. It wasn't like a great fire. Natee thought someone had painted a thin line on the horizon.

"I wonder if someone is over there?" said Natee.

Sara began to stir by stretching her legs and wings out. Natee wasn't sure what to feed her if anything at all.

"Besides pizza, do you eat anything else? You must eat something that is here," said Natee. "Maybe you could find some food on the island?"

Sara waddled over to Natee and leaned down. Natee climbed up on her back once again. She held on tight as Sara opened her wings and began to flap vigorously. Then Sara began to run down the beach until she was airborne.

They flew close to the water and straight toward the island. Natee could see from time to time the island getting larger. It was a rock island that stuck out of the water with a few trees that sprawled up the hillside.

Natee couldn't see where the smoke had been coming from until after Sara had landed. When Natee slid off of Sara she saw a building with marble pillars. At the front were steps that led up to bronze doors. There was a copper dome on top of the building that shimmered with the day light.

Natee walked up the many steps to the bronze doors. She knocked. There was no answer. She knocked again, and still no answer. Natee grabbed the heavy handled door and pulled. The large door opened with ease and a gush of cool air came rushing out.

The foyer was all wall to wall marble. The ceiling was hand painted of beautiful magical creatures. Natee knew some of them like the unicorn and the dragon. She guessed that one might be a griffin. The sound of her boots echoed as she walked. From the foyer Natee had three choices to go, all of which had steps that led to an elevated floor.

Natee looked down to the right. Then she turned and looked down to the left. The way forward looked the same. With her magic wand pointed straight out in front of her, she proceeded forward up the steps and down the long passage. Her boots still echoed as she walked on the marbled floor. "I'm sure someone knows I'm here by now."

From a hidden door that was in the wall, a woman came out behind Natee. Her presence wasn't known to Natee for a while. It was when she happened to stop and looked around that Natee notice her.

"Who are you?" asked Natee while she pointed the wand at the woman.

"Don't you think I should be asking that question?" said the woman. "And give me that wand before you hurt someone with it."

"Sorry I don't think that is a good idea that I give you my only protection in this realm," said Natee.

"We are still at the same question. Who are you?" asked the woman.

"I'm Natee. I'm a powerful witch."

"Oh yes, yes of course, you're a powerful witch," snickered the woman. "And how old are you, Natee, twelve, thirteen?

"How does my age diminish my power to you?" asked Natee.

"Power didn't get you into this realm," said the woman noticing Natee's black cape.

"But you'll need the strongest magical power ever to get back out. What brings you here in the first place?"

"I'm just here to find a friend's amulet," said Natee.

"Oh, is it the shattered amulet you're referring to? The one that is missing a sliver?" asked the woman.

Natee still holding the wand at the woman began to get nervous. She tried to come up with an answer that wouldn't give her away.

"It might be. I'm not sure what condition it may be in after all these years."

"You don't have to play mind games with me. I came here quite some time ago to find the forbidden knowledge about the whereabouts of the door to leave this universe. Mukul asked me if I happened to find his amulet if I would bring it back," said the woman. "I was young then, but this place is more powerful than anyone imagined. You can get in, it's getting out that is impossible."

"I'll just go back the way I came," said Natee.

"You won't get past the flowing water of the river. It was easy to pass through the pools this way because the water flows this way. I tried passing back through the pools by holding onto a rock the same way I got here. The current is too strong," said the woman.

Natee lowered the wand but did not put it away. "The trolls said you made it out."

"They thought I did because I fooled them into thinking that. I fooled the whole realm so I could hide here and not be bothered by those hideous creatures that come out after darkness. They don't come over here to the island. We're safe in here," said the woman.

"Can you help me get the amulet and I need to leave before darkness comes," said Natee.

"I told you there is no way out of the realm," said the woman.

Natee stood up straight, looked at the old woman and said, "And I said I'm a powerful witch. Mukul made sure of that."

The woman laughed and then pointed down the marbled hall. "You had best come with me. I have information about Mukul that no one knows. This kind of information is only kept in the Realm of Forbidden Magic. It's the secrets that people take to their grave."

Natee followed the woman down the hall to an opening into a large room. In the middle of the room was a pedestal where a statue should be. The woman passed her hand across the flat marble plate of the pedestal.

An image of Mukul appeared. "Listen and watch, my young foolish girl and learn who Mukul really is."

She watched and heard not only the conversations, but what Mukul was thinking.

It was very late in the night and Mukul knew a knock on his door was about to happen.

"I need your help," said the man. "My daughter, she has the fever."

"And you want me to break the law and cure her? Is my life worth less than your daughter's?" asked Mukul.

"Please I'm begging you, don't let my child fall victim to this mad man. You are our only hope," said the man.

"Yes," Mukul thought. "This is my chance to steal a soul."

The little girl was lying in her straw stuffed bed with hand woven blankets wrapped around her. Mukul pulled from his rucksack a bottle and pulled the cork stopper out. With his finger he rubbed the death poison on her forehead while chanting a spell.

"Farquest, bezellonus, yetella. Begone from this one and inflect no other. Nor sister, nor brother or father." Then he whispered into the girl's ear, *"Sleep eternally my sweet."*

"No, I can't believe this can be true of Mukul," said Natee.

The girl lay still in her straw bed. She was dead and his plans for immortality were just starting.

On the morning of a total eclipse in land of Ugarit, Mukul was tied down on the stone table. The judge read the charge against Mukul "You murdered a child with magic!"

"Not guilty," yelled Mukul. Only He knew what he was really guilty of. He was going to take that secret to his death and release the little girl's soul from bondage within him to fool death. He waited for death to come.

"This is not what Mukul had told me. He was trying to save that girls life," said Natee.

"Wait, before you impose sentence hear me out," said a woman that just appeared in the witch's circle. "I am Euphoria a witch that lives in Camden. They waited until that girl was near death before asking for Mukul's help. They used him as the match to light the fuse of revolt. His life should be spared for he did only what he knew was right." The woman hung her head and cried while the sentence was read.

The judge spoke with a booming voice. "It is by the council that you Mukul should live in torment of your deeds until you are vanquished by a pure hearted act. Your amulet will be crushed into shards and the smallest piece will remain with you. The rest of your amulet will be placed in the Realm of Forbidden Magic.

"No, just kill me,' yelled Mukul. *"I'm guilty, I'm guilty, I'm guiltyeeeeee."*

The image faded and Natee turned to the woman. "You're Euphoria. You tried to save his life but caused him to be cursed instead.

The woman hung her head, "Yes I'm Euphoria. I didn't know that he had that girl's soul hidden inside him. When I did find out, I decided to find his amulet and also the door out of this universe. I would fix his life and mine as well."

"Now can I have his amulet?" asked Natee.

"Not yet there is more," said Euphoria. She waved her hand over the marble surface once again.

Mukul was sitting in his shack writing in a book. His thoughts were speaking out. "I'll fix Shasta's little magical mistake and separate her two magic's. I'll keep her white magic for myself and pass on to her child her black magic. That child will be the one that will go into the Realm of Forbidden Magic and retrieve my amulet."

Another memory appeared for Natee to see and hear. "Once I have my amulet back I will finish what I started, and I'll arrange for little Natee to go to a witch's coven. When they find out that she has all black magic, their stupid governing rules will make them take care of her with a fiery death. They're burn her for being a sorceress before she can do any harm."

Natee stood there in shock. "Mukul used my great, great grandmother to make me a sorceress. And now he is using me to get his amulet. He knows that if the witch's coven finds out I'm a sorceress they will destroy me leaving him with Shasta's amulet and his amulet. What is he going to do with that little girl's soul?"

"I don't know, I can only imagine what kind of immortality spell he has planned." said Euphoria.

Natee was furious. She stomped around the room making the sound of her boots echo. She clenched her fists and her teeth. She wanted to lash out at him, but he wasn't there to hear anything that she wanted to say.

"I want that amulet. I will find a way out of this realm. He has made one too many mistakes with other people's lives," said Natee.

"Don't go making mistakes of your own. First, I wish you all the luck in finding a way out of here. If you can't, come back here and we will deal with whatever will come next. Second, if you do find a way out find a good powerful witch that will help you with your black magical powers. Just because your power is black doesn't make you a bad witch," said Euphoria.

She slid open a little door in the pedestal and pulled out a black pouch. "It's in here. I kept it here after I found all the pieces. It was scattered all over the realm."

Natee took the black pouch and gave Euphoria a hug. "Thank you, and if there is any way to let you know how to get out of here I will let you know."

Euphoria handed Natee a folded piece of paper. "For what it's worth, here is where the door out of this universe is located."

Natee stuffed the paper into her bag of gold coins. "You never know, that information might be useful for something," thought Natee.

"It would be best if you waited until morning to leave. You wouldn't get to the pool before darkness comes," said Euphoria. "I'll show you a place to sleep tonight."

Euphoria helped Natee ready herself for bed. She took Natee's black cape and neatly put it in a hidden drawer in the wall.

Natee didn't do much sleeping that night. She removed her boots and quietly walked down the other two marble halls, opening doors and going through rooms.

Very early the next morning just as the sky was lighting up Natee made her way out of the marble building. Natee didn't notice that she had forgotten her black cape. Waiting outside was Sara the dragon. "How strong are you?" Natee knew that was a moot question.

Natee stood there talking to Sara explaining her plan of getting back to the entrance to the realm.

Then Natee climbed onto Sara's back. Sara began to run down the path to the water while flapping her wings. Just before the edge of the waves, Sara gave a big push down with her wings and lifted her hind legs off the ground.

Sara flew swiftly and followed the river back to the pool where Natee emerged from after letting go of the rock. Sara swooped down toward the pool where the water was flowing out. She then shot straight up into the air as high as she could go. Sara flipped over and began to dive down with her wings tucked in close to her body.

Natee hung on tight with her eyes closed. At the last second Sara made a short sound to let Natee know to hold her breath. The two of them plunged hard into the pool. Down into the darkness of the water they went.

Chapter Eighteen
Blood Bath

After a full week of Natee being gone, Howard and Melissa stormed into the Moonlite and Spiders Crossquarter Festival glow-in-the-dark supply store. "Where are my daughter and that magician Mukul," exclaimed Melissa.

Cyndi Whetstone stared at Melissa for the longest time before answering. "Did you try the Poison Apple Tavern?"

"Where is Agnes or Harriet?" asked Howard.

"Across the street I imagine in their potion shop," said Cyndi Whetstone.

Melissa looked around to realize that she had in fact walked into the wrong quirky shop. She didn't say a word, but turned and walked out the door.

Howard shrugged his shoulders, "Sorry," he said as he walked out.

Agnes was in the shop alone when Melissa walked in. "Every day for the past week you have told me to be patient that you would find her. Where is my daughter?"

"She is in the Realm of Forbidden Magic, and we are working on a plan to rescue her," said Agnes.

"Rescue her?" insisted Melissa. "Are you telling me she is in trouble?"

The door of the shop opened with Howard walking in just at the time Melissa was asking her question.

"Harriet and I are going to get Natee out of the realm. It's not a very nice place to go," said Agnes. "Your concern is well noted. All of us are on edge because she hasn't showed up yet. We had to wait for the other entrance to the realm to open up for us."

While Melissa was listening and fuming, Howard was fiddling with an object from the gag display. "Don't touch anything. You don't know what it might do," said Melissa.

Agnes continued, "For right now I need you to go down to the Poison Apple Tavern. My husband Franklin is there with a wizard from the governing body of the magical world. He needs to talk to you about Mukul. If you are looking for justice, this is the man that will bring Mukul to trial for any wrong doings."

Agnes directed them down the street as she closed and locked up the potion shop then disappeared.

Harriet was at the magical medical ward visiting Winston. "Just a couple more days then I can take you home."

Winston talked for the first time since the magical accident. With a gruff voice he strained to say, "Must not let bottle out of sight. Bad…" His voice crackled. "…inside."

"Shhh," said Harriet. "We won't touch the bottle. I won't let it leave your side.

Agnes appeared at the door to the ward and motioned to Harriet. "Are you ready to go?"

"I thought I lost him, I just didn't have the courage to tell him where I'm going now," said Harriet.

Howard and Melissa walked through the two wood doors of the tavern with the flaming sign above it. It was late afternoon and the usual crowd was in there after working on the zeppelin assembly line all day.

Franklin spotted them and directed them to the back room, "Come and sit with us."

They walked into a large room with a quant fireplace and privacy from the other part of the tavern. "This is James Candlewick and his wife Stephanie. They're from England. This is Peter Candlewick and his wife Katee, your neighbors from across the road. They are Wesley's parents.

"We don't want to intrude on your family gathering," said Melissa.

"We are here for you, Mrs. Keystone. Since Winston has been laid up in the hospital we have been working on the proposal that you had seen in that newsmagazine and what Mukul has been doing for the past hundred years. I need to talk to you about your family history," said James.

Franklin said, "James here is a Clairvoyantologist."

"We don't need our fortunes read," said Melissa.

"Please, Mr. and Mrs. Keystone sit down. We'll have a nice dinner and some entertaining conversations," said James.

Food and drinks were brought in. The atmosphere was chilling to the Keystones. It felt like a Séance was on the menu for dinner.

"Mr. Keystone, where exactly did you pickup that newsmagazine?" asked James.

Howard began to tell the story of how they were looking for a small town to move to. "On no particular day, this unusual newsmagazine comes in the company mail. Nobody at my work wanted to even touch it. I looked at the cover and picked it up just to flip through it."

"No particular day? Can you give me more details? What day of the week did it come? Was it a holiday of some kind?" asked James.

Melissa said, "Watch it, he baiting you. This is how they get information to turn around on you to tell you your future."

"Mrs. Keystone, what I am asking has to do with why you are here in Broomstick, and what your daughter is doing in the Realm of Forbidden Magic. I investigate causes and effects in one's life. Do you think you are here just by coincident? That you may have out of the blue discovered a great deal on a ranch house and bakery? Mrs. Keystone, you have been manipulated by persons in the magical world all your life without you knowing it. Wouldn't you like to know who they are and stop it?" said James.

"I do," said Howard. "Um, it was a Tuesday the twenty ninth of March. I don't recall any holiday though."

"Oh yes, this is fitting, it's the festival of smoke and mirrors day. It's the day that one can do something and cover their tracks with illusions. The perpetrator of sending this newsmagazine to your office did it under the guise of that day and most likely had a charm on it that only you would be interested in looking at it," said James. "Very ingenious."

"It isn't so ingenious now, the bakery is burnt down, a man is in the hospital, my daughter is a witch, and when she returns from wherever she is at now, we're leaving." said Melissa.

Franklin jumped into the conversation with, "Your daughter

was a witch when she was born. That had nothing to do with you coming to Broomstick."

"Incorrect, on your last statement, Franklin, it has everything to do with them coming to Broomstick," said James. "That is why I must ask you some very strange questions."

James fired questions at Melissa about her family history. Where she grew up, what spells she remembers Shasta doing, words or phrases that she might have used, and people that her family associated with that might have been connected to the magical world.

"What do you think caused the genetic skip in your family?" asked James.

"We bred them out. None of us wanted anything to do with that crazy stuff Shasta was doing. When she died we thought that was the last of that old supernaturalism cult," stated Melissa with a little snobbishness thrown in.

"Tell me about when you tried those spells in Shasta shadow book. What particular one were you trying to do?" asked James.

Melissa looked dumbfounded. Other than Mukul popping up with that box, no one knew what she had done when she took those things. "I, um, I don't think I want to tell a room full of strangers what I tried. I did find out that I'm not one of you. I'm not a witch."

"You knew that before you tried the spells, why did you try anyway? And how did you know that one particular spell didn't work?" pinned James.

"You're guessing. You have no idea what I tried," said Melissa.

"You tried to get a better position in your company with a particular spell. You know which one I'm referring to. It's the power of suggestion and influence spell. You collected your boss's hair for weeks to do that spell, and nothing happened. Then you blew your temper at your boss for discrimination and got fired," explained James.

"Fired, you said you quit to pursue a better job," said Howard.

"That doesn't make me a witch," said Melissa.

"No it doesn't make you a witch. It did, however get someone's attention on how to influence your dissensions in the future. They knew what you wanted exactly by you doing that spell. It was a window into your eyes," explained James.

"It was Mukul. He said he was always there watching us," said Melissa.

"Sorry, he is not the one that has been manipulating you. Since I've been talking to you, I've changed my direction of thought to another." said James.

The whole room stopped eating, drinking, or moving. Their heads were turned toward James in anticipation of what he was to say next. Even the noise of the tavern had stopped.

Agnes and Harriet had just arrived at the edge of the plane that led to the Realm of Forbidden Magic. It was a dark thin line between the two realms of twilight and the outer limit.

A tight fit waited for both of them as they squeezed through the opening. "You know if we were virgins we could have used the other portal," said Harriet.

"Losing a few pounds would have made this way easier also," quipped Agnes.

They had a long walk ahead of them to get to the Unicorn Reflection Pond where Mukul said he had sent Natee.

The rush of the water around Natee was tremendous. She was holding on as hard as she could.

"I can't let go. I can't let go," she kept thinking as she was still holding her breath.

She knew time was running out. Her air was almost gone and she could feel the pressure on her chest. Her fingers began to loosen their grip as she began to fade to darkness.

Then the dragon burst out the pool straight up into the air with a loud cry. Natee breathed in air of relief. Sara flew gently down and stamped her feet on the sandy bank of the river as she came in for a landing.

Natee slid off Sara's back and fell onto the sand panting for air. She was exhausted from holding on so tight. Her hands began to cramp with pain. She knew that she couldn't lie there much longer for the sky was dimming above her.

Sara began to roar and swing her head back and forth. Natee turned over onto her stomach to look at what she was doing. Sebastian was walking up the river bank to where Natee was laying. "It's okay Sara he is a friend. His name is Sebastian."

Sara stopped her commotion and sat down for she was also exhausted from her flight through the rushing water.

"Sebastian could you have your friends bring us some food, drink, and firewood please?"

Sebastian asked, "Did you find what you were looking for?"

"Yes and a lot more," said Natee.

After the fire was burning and Natee had eaten, she drew a circle around her.

When Natee started to ask the wand to protect her, Natee realized she didn't have Shasta's magical cape.

"How am I going to get through the tunnel without my protection cape?" Natee thought.

Natee tried to clear her mind for the time being by telling Sebastian and the other trolls her story of what happened on the other side of the pool.

"And Euphoria is still trapped over on the other side," said Natee.

It was dark and the trolls scattered up into the rocks for protection. There weren't too many sounds coming from the dark. On occasion Sara would let out a burst of fire overhead.

Natee was relieved at being on this side of the fairy pool. However, she was still aware of the dangers that were still around her. She fell to sleep within her circle with both hands holding onto the wand.

She awoke to daylight brightly above in the sky. The trolls have already put a basket of fruit near her and Sara had her mouth inside a larger basket eating away.

This was the day that Natee was looking forward to and also dreaded. When she first arrived, it was on the back of a unicorn. It was very soon thereafter that the unicorn had abandoned her and went back through the tunnel. Then she made the mistake of putting her hand into the river water letting the realm know she was there.

"I'm afraid that I have one big question. Can I get passed the tunnel without the Grendels and the Harpies hearing or seeing me?" asked Natee aloud.

Sara poked Natee with her head and grunted while shooting little flames out of her mouth.

"I'm not sure what you have in mind but just standing here isn't getting me nearer to the tunnel.

Natee climbed onto Sara's back, once again grabbing on to her scales tightly.

Sara started down the river bank flapping her wings until she became airborne. She flew up and out of the canyon and by midday they were passing over the table rock that opened up the canyon.

Sara landed just before the tunnel where the unicorn had left Natee. "Are you going to take me through the tunnel?" asked Natee.

Sara shook her head, but puffed out a little flame once again. "I'm not sure what you are getting at, but I have to try. It's my only way out."

Natee hugged Sara around her scaly neck and started for the tunnel. She thought that maybe if she walked quietly through she could make it to the other side. Sara brought her head directly in front of Natee at the tunnel and blew the largest bubble of fire she could into the tunnel.

Natee got Sara's idea real quick. She started running right behind the hot fire ball. She ran and ran and didn't stop. Just about at the end of the tunnel, the fire ball smoldered out. Natee could see the light outside.

She kept running as fast as she could. It was like in her nightmare. She was running trying to fly to get away from all these monsters that were close behind her now. She could smell their rotten raw meat hot breath and feel the needle point of their claws in her back. They were ripping her clothes and snagging their claws into the skin of her back. The tunnel opening was just right there.

Natee closed her eyes and forced herself even harder to keep running as her legs were tightening up. She knew this was her last push. "Either I make it or I get eaten up by these terrible creatures."

Finely Natee stopped smelling the stench of their breaths. She opened her eyes and saw the pond that she had found the unicorn by. Totally exhausted Natee collapsed into the clear water. Her back was ripped to shreds from the creatures claws. The blood from her back bled out and changed the color of the water to a dark murky crimson. She laid there in the water with half of her face sticking out. Natee passed out.

Agnes and Harriet weren't having an easy go of it. The ground was rocky, the air was hot, and the light was a dismal brown.

"If I wanted to keep something from anyone else this would be the place to keep it at," said Harriet.

"And this isn't even the realm yet. I can't imagine that it could be worse than this, but by what has been said about it, it is," said Agnes.

In the visible distance they could see an oasis of grass and small shrubs. There was a large pond of water.

"There's the portal Mukul told us about," said Agnes.

As Agnes and Harriet got closer they saw that the water was

not crystal clear. It was a hazy brownish red. On the other side of the pond laid Natee in the water. Agnes and Harriet scurried around to the other side.

The two of them splashed into the water and grabbed Natee by her arms and shoulders and picked her up. With Natee's arms around their necks, Harriet and Agnes carried her out of the water.

"Looks like she had a busy day, I think it is time for this witch to come home," said Harriet.

Chapter Nineteen
Memories can be Nightmares

Carrying the limp girl, Agnes and Harriet materialized at the desk of the magical medical emergency ward of the Broomstick Hospital. Blood drops could be seen on the floor under Natee.

Attendants quickly came and carried Natee into a medical room laying her on her chest. The on duty witch pulled her wand out and magically removed Natee's ripped bodysuit, gloves and boots.

"The girl is dehydrated, malnourished, and has lost a lot of blood," said the witch. "What creature caused these wounds?"

"The Grendels and Harpies that protect the entrance to the Realm of Forbidden Magic," said Agnes.

The witch used a pair of tweezers and picked at one of the bleeding wounds. She removed a little gray speck with the tweezers. Then she pulled out a glass fish eye from the examining tool drawer. Under the fish eye the gray speck looked like a little limp squid.

"Was there any magical treatment given before she was brought here?" inquired the witch.

"No, we just grabbed her when we found her and came directly here," said Agnes.

"Wait a second," said Harriet. "We pulled her out of the Unicorn Reflection Pond."

The witch held up the little gray dead thing and said, "Well that was a stroke of good luck for her. If she hadn't fallen into that pond these little spores would be eating her alive right now and there would have been nothing I could have done about it."

From another drawer, the witch pulled out a flat wood stick and a jar with yellow healing suave. She began to spread the yellow suave on Natee's wounds.

Natee's eyes opened and she clenched her teeth. She sucked in air as the yellow suave stung with healing pain.

"Relax little one, I know this hurts, but it is going to take me some time to dab this on each one of your wounds," said the witch.

Natee laid there with tears in her eyes. Agnes, Harriet, and the attending witch thought it was from the pain of the suave.

Natee kept running over and over through her head what she had learned about Mukul. She thought to herself, "I trusted you. You were my mentor, my friend." Her whimpers continued even after the witch was through with the suave.

Agnes was about to leave the hospital to let Natee's parents know that they had found her. Harriet was staying behind to take care of Winston. Natee was given the next bed over.

Mukul appeared at the window to the ward staring in at Natee.

Both Agnes and Harriet trotted up to him with their wands pulled out and poked him in the chest.

"You stay away from her!" said Agnes while waving her wand in his face.

"Let me turn him into a toad and feed him to our twin Siamese floral weed seedling," said Harriet.

Mukul tried to ignore the remarks and the wand jabs. With a concerned expression he asked, "How is she?"

"That is not what you want to know," said Harriet. "Your concerned expression isn't working."

"She'll be fine as long as you don't come near her anymore. I'll let you know if she got your amulet or not. So far it looks like she didn't get past those creatures that guard the entrance," said Agnes. "Now go away!"

Mukul lowered his head and turned away from the window. He faded out of the hospital.

Mukul sat slumped in his chair inside his shack up on the top of the mountain over looking Shadow Creek Valley.

"I didn't mean for anything to happen to Natee. I love her as if she was my own granddaughter," said Mukul aloud. There was no one there to hear him say it, or so he thought.

James Candlewick appeared off to Mukul's side not quite in eye sight. "I know you didn't want Natee to be in any danger. That is why you prepared her for all possible tribulations except one. What's her name?"

Mukul didn't even move or flinch. He just answered, "Euphoria."

"How is it that she can move in and out of the Realm of Forbidden Magic?" asked James.

"She can't actually physically leave the realm. She learned over the centuries how to use her black magic to move almost ghostlike to where she wanted to be. You have to admit black magic does have some redeeming qualities.

"Euphoria could have called off those creatures from harming Natee. Any idea why she didn't?" questioned James.

"I-I don't know, jealousy perhaps. When she went to get my amulet, she got trapped inside the realm and couldn't get out. After the first century she figured out how to get out, but real time was waiting for her outside. If she tried to leave she would turn into dust," explained Mukul.

"An unfortunate set of events for the two of you. Love is powerful, but no one ever said it couldn't be cruel," said James.

"When did you figure out there was someone else involved?" asked Mukul.

"It had to do with what Melissa said about breeding magic out of the family tree. Didn't you find that strange?

"I always thought it was that mistake Shasta did just before I met her. She tried to do a reincarnation ritual. It made her black and white magic out of sync. Their powers were canceling each other out. I took advantage of that time to take her white magic side away from her. I used it for my own purposes. I also thought I could use her to go to the realm. I didn't know she had a husband," explained Mukul.

"Black magic can be used to manipulate other black magic

to stay dormant and move down the family line. Euphoria kept you from getting another girl to come after the amulet. Natee's magic was too powerful to repress for another generation. So you used this valued opportunity to get your amulet and try to help Euphoria," said James. "Do you want to talk to Natee?"

"Will those two mother hens allow it? Harriet wanted to feed me to her twin Siamese floral weed seedling," said Mukul.

Natee laid awake writing in her new shadow book about everything she learned while in the Realm of Forbidden Magic. One particular piece of information was a reincarnation spell that Euphoria had been studying.

Natee wrote, "It must be a night of new moon when the sky and magic are at their darkest hour. Prepare a witches circle of magic by carefully sweeping the ground clear of anything dead, like insects, plant twigs and leaves, and animal remains."

Natee made little diagrams and side notes. "Wear an enchanted black hooded cape. Euphoria must have stolen my black cape for this spell."

Natee knew about protections circles now. "With the blunt end of a staff draw a protective witch's circle around the cauldron filled with the ashes of the dead. Hem, Shasta had her black hooded cape in a cauldron."

"Fill in the etched magic circle with sand from an hourglass by breaking one end of the glass and slowly walking the circle pouring the sand out."

Natee turned a page as she kept writing. "At the hour of midnight, place the end of the staff in the cauldron down into the ashes. Hold the staff straight up and chant, "Ference Gusto en Debblas Zate. Reverse this one's fate. REINCARNATE!"

"Why was Euphoria interested in a reincarnation spell?"

Winston was tossing and turning in the late night with moans and groans. Natee got up out of her bed and went over to Winston. He was having a nightmare.

Natee tried to comfort him by rubbing his forehead. Instead she became aware that she could see his nightmare.

Natee began to observe his nightmare… *as he slid a key into the lock of a coffin and slowly turned the key. The tumbler turned allowing the internal dead bolt to move. Grasping the handle, Winston lifted the lid of the coffin. Suddenly an arm reached out of the coffin and the lid was ripped out of Winston's hand while being pushed opened by the occupant of the coffin. A grotesque creature clamored out of the coffin right towards Winston.*

Winston stumbled back falling into shelves and knocking off glass bottles and other various objects trying to keep on his feet. A jar with the label 'Emotions of Jack the Ripper' fell off a shelf and rolled down into a floor drain where the grating had been removed. It was lodged in the drain hole.

Clouds swirled and faces changed as his dream progressed. Natee stayed with Winston as her being there calmed him down.

When a bucket of dirty mop water was poured down the drain the clogged drain filled up. Wardcrystal had put a magical fire spell around the jar to keep anyone from touching it except him.

The water boiled and sputtered causing gasses and orange steam to bellow out of the drain. Winston yelled "GET OUT OF HERE!" He hid in the service closet waiting for it to stop. Natee watched as Winston grabbed a water hose and went back out spraying water at the drain. He pulled the grating off and stuck his hand down the drain.

He grabbed the jar and tossed it in the mop bucket and filled it with water. Magical fire was burning the building all around him. He kept the water hose on himself as he made his way out the back door to the alley. In the alley was a large glass five gallon drinking water bottle. Winston poured the dingy mop bucket water with the jar into the bottle. He melted the glass bottle neck with his wand to seal the bottle closed.

The dream ended with him looking into Natee's eyes when she said "You're Winston". Natee was surprise as Winston also woke up from his nightmare doing the same thing.

With a gruff voice, Winston whispered, "You saw it, you saw the nightmare."

Natee apologized, "It was by accident. I was just trying to calm you down from tossing in your sleep. I wasn't trying to pry into your personal thoughts,"

"You know what is in the bottle. I need to destroy it. Can't let it out ever again," said Winston with a crackling voice.

"Shhh," said Natee. "Don't talk anymore. I know where you can put it and it will never return. When we both get out of here I'll take you to where the portal is to the Outside of the Universe."

The next day Natee went home with her parents. The three of them drove away from Broomstick Hospital with Natee sitting in the far back seat up against the window.

"Natalie, I meant to say Natee," said Melissa. "Agnes told us what you tried to do. I'm sorry that you didn't even make it into that zone place. You don't have to prove to anyone that you are a witch by doing dangerous things. Just stay home and do your magical stuff in a safe place. We will support your decision on following Shasta's cult."

Natee just stared out the window. "You still don't understand. If Mukul hadn't interfered with our family you would be a witch too. And who said I didn't make it into the Realm of Forbidden Magic?"

"Agnes said when they found you, you were dehydrated, malnourished and almost mortally wounded by those creatures that guard the entrance," said Melissa trying to still comprehend all this magic world stuff.

"The witchdoctor explained that whatever I ate or drank in the realm sustained me in the realm. Once I left the realm I caught up with real time and I hadn't eaten or drank anything for the last five days," Natee tried to explain. "And yes I was almost eaten by the Grendels and Harpies."

Her two brothers were waiting at the ranch house with different attitudes toward Natee. Before they were a little apprehensive about her magical powers, now her brothers were fearful, but more sociable toward her.

They sat down as a family for dinner. Something they hadn't done since they arrived in Broomstick. The atmosphere was a chilling winter storm with everyone just staring at their plates and eating.

Natee chose this time to show what she had done in the realm. She had sitting next to her a bag from the hospital of what she had on her when she was brought in.

Out of the bag Natee pulled the bag of gold coins and sat it next to her dad's plate. "Here dad, this will help rebuild the bakery faster."

Howard set down his fork and opened the bag. "Are these coins pure gold?"

"I think so, but you'll have to ask Mr. Wisestone when he gets out of the hospital."

Then Natee pulled out her black bodysuit that was ripped to shreds with dried blood soaked into the fabric. "This is for you mom, just to show you how they found me."

The entire family stared with frozen expressions at the bodysuit when Natee held it up and showed the back was ripped to shreds.

The awkward moment was broken with a knock at the door. Natee moved away from the table as no one else was moving. When she opened the door, James and Mukul were standing there.

"May we come in, Natee," said James. "I don't mean to bother you. I know you just got home, but the three of us need to discuss some things about recent events."

"Um, come on in. We can talk in the den," said Natee.

After they were in the den, James waved his wand to seal the room.

Natee stood there with her arms folded across her chest trying not to look at Mukul.

James began, "There are some people in the magical world that think you never got into the Realm of Forbidden Magic. The three of us know that you did and you retrieved the shattered amulet from Euphoria."

Natee didn't blink an eye although she was taken back at the news. "Then you can guess that she showed me who you really are, what you wanted to do centuries ago, and how you planned to use and dispose of me."

"Natee, The events of my memories you saw had been tampered with by Euphoria," said Mukul.

"You used my family to make me a witch with only black magic. I was just a pawn in your dirty little game of obtaining your magic back," said Natee with tears in her eyes and anger in her voice.

"Yes it started that way, but I..." Mukul was interrupted by Natee.

"I don't want to hear anything you have to say. I loved you. You were my mentor, my friend." Natee stopped to catch her breath. "You can just go to blazes," yelled Natee with tears streaming down her face.

"That's a nice way to say it, but that place doesn't exist in our dogma," said Mukul.

"Well it should. People like you belong there," said Natee.

James interrupted the tossing of insults with, "Before you pass judgment on him Natee, I think you need some more facts."

James started at the beginning when Mukul was trying to save the girls life and that of the village from the fever. "It was Drake that knew how to spread the fever and kept certain people from catching it. Mukul knew all this, he just couldn't prove it. The little girl was a trap. He tried to work fast to save the girl before Drake and his men showed up."

As the story was told to her, Natee realized that what Euphoria had shown her had been tampered with to show a dreadful version.

"Euphoria was the one that started the magical problems in your family by causing Shasta to make a mistake in her spell.

She also suppressed the magic for as long as she could to prevent anyone from having the magic needed to enter the realm."

James concluded with the biggest surprise to Natee, "Euphoria controlled the night creatures of the realm. You weren't supposed to succeed. You amazed her when you showed up on the island. You stunned her when you made it back to the tunnel. She was going to let you be killed in the tunnel by her creatures to stop you from leaving with the amulet. They were waiting for you. She didn't expect that dragon to do what she did to help you get out."

Natee turned to Mukul. "I believed her. She had me convinced that you were the dirty wizard with self-centered aspirations of power. I'm sorry for what I said. I do still love you."

"I know you do. Don't think too badly of Euphoria. Centuries of being in that realm and never allowed to leave it caused her to hate more and love less. Black magic does that to people. She didn't want anyone to get my amulet for me. She had me to herself indirectly," said Mukul.

After they hugged each other Natee handed the little pouch with his shattered amulet inside. "She said it was all there. I hope she didn't lie about that."

When Natee, James, and Mukul came out of the den, Agnes and Harriet were there.

Mukul held up his hands in defense. "Now ladies, James arranged this meeting."

Agnes said, "That is not what we are here for. Natee it is time for you to get ready for your witch's coven and birthday party."

Chapter Twenty
The Witch's Coven

Natee was taken to the magical broom production building. Inside the nymphs were waiting to give her a complete makeover. They had a bath waiting for her. She removed her clothes and stepped into the large tub of warm water.

Two nymphs gently washed Natee in pure spring water and used a pink clay scrub with palm oil to cleanse her skin. Another nymph washed her hair in sweet almond oil shampoo.

She was dried with a velvet rose petal towel. It gathered up every drop of water. Natee's hair was brushed out to a silky smooth softness with a unicorn's tail hair brush.

Her witch's robe, hat, stockings and slippers were made of white silk.

Natee sat in a chair in front of a mirror as the nymphs applied makeup to her face. They started with soft face powder and gently brushed it around giving her a natural color.

The nymphs went with a dark mysterious look for her eyes as they shaded her eyelids and accented her eyebrows with a slight upturn at the end.

Her lip color was feathered to blend her mouth into her face keeping the accent on her eyes.

"It's time to go," said a nymph who escorted Natee to the clearing.

Everyone was standing at the clearing just before the trees that led to the witch's coven circle. Natee walked past them as each one greeted her and wished her good fortunes. Her parents hugged her. Peter and Katee Candlewick were standing there with Wesley.

"You look very beautiful Natee," said Wesley as he turned red for saying it in front of his parents.

Natee leaned over and kissed him on the cheek. "Thank you Wesley. Will you dance with me at my party? You are still my boyfriend, you know," whispered Natee in his ear.

James and Stephanie Candlewick both gave her a hug. Natee cringed with icy chills when James touched her.

There was a crowd from the town watching as she got to the last person in the line. Mukul was standing there with his staff that had the globe on top with Shasta's white magic amulet inside.

"I've been waiting for this day ever since I was asked to be your mentor by Shasta. Listen, I have something very important to do. I finally figured out about the pure hearted act. I have been waiting for centuries for someone to do a pure hearted act for me, when all this time it was I that needed to do the act. I had the keys to unlock the jail all along and didn't even know I had them," said Mukul.

"But I did the pure hearted act, I got your amulet from the Realm of Forbidden Magic for you," said Natee.

"And what a loyal act of true love that was. In return I want to give you a birthday present. You will be receiving my staff. I won't need it on my journey. You have been the granddaughter I never had. But that is not true. To me you have been my granddaughter all along," said Mukul with tears in his eyes.

He held out his hand and placed the orange amulet in it. The one shard emerged from his scar and joined with the amulet. Mukul's spider scar disappeared. His orange amulet now complete, Mukul placed the amulet into his right hand.

Mukul handed the staff over to Agnes.

"You're not leaving. You're supposed to protect me," said Natee.

Mukul knelt down to eye level with Natee. "I have to go and get Euphoria and take her and this child to Nirvana personally. My pure hearted act is to retrieve the one that has always loved me from an eternal life of misery. You understand don't you?"

"Yes, I understand," said Natee not wanting to.

"Now go and have a great witch's coven and be the witch that would make your great, great grandmother proud," said Mukul.

Natee started walking away with Agnes, and then she looked back at Mukul as she walked to the grove of trees and smiled. He didn't hear her, but he read her lips when she said, "I love you Grandfather."

At the circle were eleven witches, Harriet Wisestone, Stephanie Candlewick, Penelope Münter, Cindy Münter, Cindy's twin daughters April Castlerock and May Münter, Mary Pride, Wanda Whetstone, Agnes' triplet daughters Cyndi, Mindy, and Wendy.

The drawn circle has not been completed. Agnes directed Natee to go into the center of the circle. Harriet handed Agnes the ceremonial witch's broom. She stepped into the circle and drew the closing arc.

Natee stood there thinking about how she out of instinct for symbolic protection drew those circles around her while in the realm.

"The witch's circle is complete, but not yet sealed," said Agnes. Mary stepped out of the circle of witches and began to fill in the drawn circle with rock salt. The other eleven chanted in unison.

"Close the circle. Seal it tight. For only witches are present tonight. What is said in the circle and what is done in the circle, becomes the circle. The Sisters of the Q are but just a few."

Natee stood there silent as the grave. Her makeup didn't show how pale she felt. Mary was back in place and Agnes proceeded.

She held up in front of her the ceremonial broom. "As it was in the beginning, it shall be forever and a day. A witch is a witch to her dying day,"

They all repeated in unison. "As it was in the beginning, it shall be forever and a day. A witch is a witch to her dying day,"

Natee was more frighten inside, now. "I'm not a witch. I am a sorceress because of my black magic."

Agnes continued, "Catch the spirit. Seize the wind. Feel the magic we have within. We have the power to control the world. Instead we chose to protect what nature has unfurled."

Agnes laid down the broom in front of her. "I am the guardian of all that is right".

Mary opened an old book and read, "My child, my home, my comfort, my stone."

The book was passed around the circle with each reading from it. When the book got to Penelope, she opened the book and read,

"What is not ours cannot be taken. What we hold true cannot be forsaken."

The book was passed to Agnes where she handed the book to Natee with a quill. "This is your time to share with us your experience in the Realm of Forbidden Magic. Then write a simple notation that describes what you have learned."

Natee began to tell her story. The twelve witches listen with intense interest. They nodded with approval of her finding out about the protection circle. She finished her story with what she had thought, as she fell into the Unicorn Reflection Pond. "When the water flowed around me, I felt newness surround me. I was no longer a little girl. Just before I passed out I felt the unicorn licking my wounds and saying to me, 'The eyes of true love will reflect your soul'."

Natee shrugged her shoulders. "But I don't know what that means."

Natee wrote in the book as she said, "A great fairy told me to 'Ignore the obvious, capitalize on the impervious'."

May Münter said, "That is what you need to do with what the unicorn said."

Natee handed the book back to Agnes and smiled. All her fears have vanished. Agnes then held out Mukul's magical staff with the globe at Natee.

"Hold out your left hand," said Agnes.

The globe touched Natee's palm and a flash of golden light with blue sparks surrounded her hand. Shasta's white amulet moved from the globe to Natee. An aura of lights enveloped her as the two magic's combined together once again.

Natee felt a surge of pureness rush through suppressing the

harden black magic she was born with to a whimper. Agnes handed her the staff.

Agnes then handed her Shasta's wand. "You'll need your wand for the ending ceremony."

"My wand, this is my wand? This is my wand! I have a magic wand and a magical staff." Natee held them both up and waved them around.

Harriet and Stephanie moved apart to allow Natee into the circle. They all held their wands in the air. Natee followed what they were doing.

They began to sing and dance as the circle rotated counter clockwise. Agnes picked up the ceremonial broom and as they dance around she swept the circle away. The broom vanished as the last of the circle was erased.

Just before the thirteen witches left the secluded woods Natee asked, "What does the Q stand for in the 'Sisters of the Q'?"

Everyone looked around at each other. Harriet answered, "We are the Sisters of the Quăir. The book we read from and you wrote in is our shadow book of the coven. It is a very powerful book indeed. It protects us, provides us with magic that has been passed down from members long past, and it connects us as one to one another."

The witches smiled with enchanting grins at Natee as they walked out of the woods.

Natee knew there are no secrets anymore.

It seemed to Natee like the whole town was at her thirteenth birthday party, except one. Agnes and Harriet with the help of the other witches transformed the town's cemetery with decorations of balloons, flowers, flags, and an all you can eat buffet. At the end of the table was an enormous three tiered birthday cake with thirteen of the biggest black candles Natee had ever seen.

"Black candles, you used black candles on her birthday cake? What were you thinking?" asked Agnes to Harriet.

"Remember years ago you had me order black candles for the jinxing party? We still have two crates of those candles slowly melting into a large square with wicks," answered Harriet. "Besides it matches my hair and makeup I did for Winston. He should be here shortly. Oh there he is now."

Franklin was pushing Winston in a wheel chair up to where Harriet was standing. "Just for a couple days," said Winston. "Then I'll be walking again."

All Harriet could do was put her arms around him and said, "Hiya Winston." Then she sat on his lap and kissed him over and over.

Music came from the organ in the mortuary and was accompanied by some of the permanent residences of the cemetery. Natee found Wesley and said, "How about that dance?"

Wesley turned red. "I don't know how to dance."

"Neither do I. Let's just follow what the adults are doing," said Natee.

As they danced Wesley and Natee smiled at each other and laughed when they made mistakes. Natee stopped dancing when she saw her mirrored reflection in Wesley's eyes.

She thought to herself, "May had said, 'That is what you need to do with what the unicorn said.' The fairy said, 'Ignore the obvious, capitalize on the impervious.' And the unicorn said, 'The eyes of true love will reflect your soul'."

"What's wrong? Did I step on your feet?" asked Wesley.

"No, you didn't step on my feet," said Natee and smiled at Wesley with enlightenment.

Wesley stared into Natee's eyes and saw a two tiered shadowed silhouette of Natee. The front silhouette was black with her white eyes beaming at him. Surrounding the black shadow was a shimmering aura of pure white.

Wesley saw his reflection in the eyes of the black silhouette. He got a creepy feeling down his spine like she had just ripped his heart out of his chest to keep for her very own.

Natee this time asked, "Is everything alright?"

"I saw an image of you and me in your eyes. It was like I was seeing myself inside your soul." Now looking at her, he wondered what just changed about her. She looked different to him and strangely, still the same. He also felt different.

"Mind if I cut in," said Howard. "I promise I won't keep her from you too long."

That moment of not being with Natee answered his questions through his emotions. "I haven't called her my girlfriend."

Wesley went over to his parents nervously with his hands in his pockets. "Someone took away your girlfriend?" Joked Peter. "I'm sure she'll be back."

"Dad, when did you know?" asked Wesley.

"Know what, Wesley?" inquired Peter.

"When you liked mom, I mean a whole lot," said Wesley.

"Oh I see. You want to know if you should let Natee know that you like her a lot, is that it?" said Peter.

Peter got down on one knee to be level with Wesley. "My advice to you is to tell her now, not when it is too late and someone else has taken her heart."

While Natee and her dad danced he said, "I've been talking to Winston Wisestone. Those gold coins are called wizens. They're worth millions, but only in the magical world. You can open an account at The Wizard's Bank with them. You're rich Natee."

"Now you can buy and build your bakery, Dad. What about Mom, is she okay living here?"

"We have a few things to work on, but yeah she is okay with it, I think," said Howard.

Natee finished her dance with her dad and walked over to the Candlewicks. Wesley said, "I think they want you to cut your birthday cake".

Natee grabbed Wesley's hand, "Let's go and cut my birthday cake then."

As they were walking over to where the cake was Wesley stopped Natee by pulling on her hand. "What is it Wesley?"

"I-I want to ask you, would you be my girlfriend?" asked Wesley.

Natee looked at Wesley for a moment. "I guess I took that for granted when I said that you were my boyfriend. This is different though, you asking me that is."

Natee looked at Wesley and said, "Yes, I will be your girlfriend." Then she grabbed his hand again and headed for the cake.

Natee stood there while everyone sang happy birthday to her. She cut the cake and was helped by Harriet to pass out the cake.

Melissa turned to Howard, "Look at Natee."

"Yes isn't she beautiful in her white silk witch's outfit," said Howard.

"Look again, Howard. Look at the whole scene. Don't you see it?" said Melissa.

"I see Natee cutting her cake and people congratulating her..." Then he saw what Melissa was trying to point out. There was George Düben standing behind Wesley standing next to Natee in her white witch's gown with Kizee Wisestone on Natee's other side."

Howard was still not seeing the magical world even when it is right in front of him, or he prefers to ignore it.

"Howard, in there world it is called tying the knot. They are marrying our daughter to that young boy! Howard, do something!"

Chapter Twenty One
And they Cried

Mukul made his way into the entrance of the Realm of Forbidden Magic. He walked the same path that Agnes and Harriet had taken and returned with Natee. He could see in the brown sand and rock the black spots of Natee's blood.

He picked up one of the rocks and held it in his hand. He cried. He cried for what he had put Natee through. He cried for the little girl's soul he had stolen. He cried for Euphoria and her being trapped in this realm. And he cried for his lack of understanding of what a pure hearted act meant.

Mukul carried that blood stained rock with him as he made his way to the entrance to the tunnel where he waited for Euphoria.

Euphoria easily passed through the pools from one side to the other. Euphoria used her magic to stop the flow of the water. She didn't have to hold her breath or cling on for her life. This had been what she figured out after a century of being trapped. Euphoria simply told the fairy to stop the water.

Euphoria had been so angry at herself for being so stupid that she turned her anger into power over the realm. She was Queen Euphoria to those terrible flesh eating monsters.

When she learned to project herself outside of the realm, she went to Mukul in his shack up on top of the mountain. "Come to the realm and stay here with me. We can be together forever. After all it was my love for you that made me come here in the first place to retrieve your amulet." She became even angrier when he wouldn't come.

"No, it wouldn't be right for this girl's soul to endure that. I must find a way to get her to Nirvana, even if that means I have to take her there myself," said Mukul.

Natalie Keystone, that name tasted sour in Euphoria' mouth. During the years that Mukul spent raising Natee from a small child, she would project herself and watch them together.

Euphoria could see it in Mukul's eyes. She knew that Natee was his little baby girl, and had taken her place in his heart.

Euphoria also knew that someday Mukul would send Natee after the amulet. "I'll take care of her. I'll turn her against him. Even trap her here with me. If I can't have him, he won't have her."

Now it was all for nothing. She had lost. Lost her life, lost her magic, and lost the one thing that she loved the most, her true love. Mukul said it very plainly to her the day after Natee came back from the realm. Euphoria appeared in her ghostly form in his shack. Mukul sat there crying in self-pity for what he had done.

"You tried to kill my granddaughter. You have turned wicked with 'Black Magic' as your lover. I am willing to give my life to take this girl's soul personally to Nirvana. I am going to give Natee my amulet and leave you to rot in your realm."

She left Mukul alone in his shack and lay on the marble floor of her prison and cried. At first she cried for all the wrong reasons, selfishness, pity, and hatred for the universe for doing this to her.

Then she cried for the little girl's soul that had been trapped within Mukul. She cried for Mukul as he had been tormented all these centuries with his guilt. Finally she cried for Natee and what she had tried to do to her, corrupt her against Mukul, and then tried to kill her.

After a very long cry, Euphoria went back to the shack and remorsefully asked, "Mukul, when you are ready to go to Nirvana, I want to go with you. I want your forgiveness," said Euphoria.

"When I am ready, I will call to you with my decision if I forgive you or not," said Mukul. "I have my granddaughter I must take care of first."

After Mukul saw Natee go off to her witch's coven, He called out to Euphoria. "I'm coming to take you with me. I'll meet you at the Unicorn Reflection Pond."

At the tunnel Euphoria held her head up wearing Shasta's black protection cape and walked out of the Realm of Forbidden Magic through the tunnel where the Grendels had flesh falling off of their muscled skeleton figures and burning acid drooled from their mouths. Hanging above her were the Harpies with their bony arms with feathered wings and claws. Not a single one moved.

Mukul stood at the Unicorn Reflection Pond outside the entrance to the Realm of Forbidden Magic. Euphoria walked up to Mukul.

When they kissed, Euphoria bit Mukul's lip to make it bleed. Just before they turned into their prospective piles of ash Euphoria said to Mukul, "Throw me into the pond before it's too late."

"It's already too late for the both of us. My curse is broken. I will die now."

"No, Mukul you don't understand. I did a reincarnation spell as I came out of the realm. Quickly, throw me into the pond."

Mukul held Euphoria as she struggled to get loose. They turned into piles of ash.

In their ashes lay three items. In Mukul's ashes were the orange amulet and the blood stained rock that Mukul had picked up.

Euphoria's ashes contained her dark green amulet and two orange slivers. Lying gently on the ground was Shasta's protection cape.

It was the day after Natee's birthday party when a crowd of witches and wizards gathered in front of the Wisestone's house. The noise was loud enough that it got Edna Brown's attention two houses down.

"What is going on," Edna barked.

"Winston is home from the hospital," said Bee as she and her two sisters that live next door came out to join the crowd.

There was music and dancing when Winston appeared in his front yard. Harriet came out of the house and the cheering got to an incredible loud roar. This made Winston and Harriet so happy they cried.

For some strange reason the crowd quieted down and opened up for someone to walk through. Murmurs and whispers passed through the crowd as two people walked up to the front of the house.

Winston and Harriet were shocked as Mr. and Mrs. Wisestone walked up to them.

"Son, we owe you a great apology," said Winston's father. "We lost you once as our son, then we thought we lost you again before we could reconcile. Your mother and I ask for you and Harriet to forgive us."

There weren't any words spoken from Winston and Harriet. The four of them hugged and cried. And then they hugged their granddaughter Kizee and cried some more.

The news of what the parents said spread through the crowd. The roar of cheering started up again, with music playing and everyone dancing.

That was it. There was no more trying to control the town of Broomstick. Celebrations broke out all over. The Wisestone family was taken from one side of town to the other until they were standing on the porch of the McDermit's house.

Agnes hadn't even got out of bed yet. The witch's coven and the birthday party drained her. Franklin peered out of the window at the front of their house.

"Agnes, Winston and Harriet are here. With, I think, his parents and the rest of the town."

Agnes dragged herself out of the bed and pulled on a black robe. Franklin opened the door with Agnes looking like death warmed over.

Then Agnes looked at Winston's parents with a curious expression. Winston said, "Agnes, Franklin. I would like you to meet my parents."

Harriet whispered in Agnes' ear, "I'll explain later. It's good news."

Agnes and Franklin excused themselves for a short time and got dressed. The crowd, the Wisestone's, and the McDermits were swept away to celebrations all over town.

Agnes and Harriet laughed and cried all day.

It was the end of the Keystone's vacation. Melissa was getting her suitcase packed for the trip home. "I'll be glad to get out of this nutty town. It will be easier to put up with one witch in the family then to deal with a whole town of them."

Howard didn't exactly move too quickly in getting his things together. He fidgeted and moved some things around.

"You need to get a move on," said Melissa. "It is best for Natee to get her out of here. You saw that big party last night. They'll have those two kids married before they are out of junior high school. You don't know what weird mating practices they might have. I met a woman last night that wasn't witch. Her husband had accidently got them pulled into this screwy town. She told me things that would curl your coattail. Edna Brown seems like she is the only sane person in this town."

"I'm glad you made a friend here, because I quit my job a month ago" said Howard.

"YOU WHAT?" said Melissa. "No, I'm not going to live here. You are going to call them right now and asked, no, beg for your job back."

"I was talking to Winston last night. If we agreed to stay, The

Mayor's office and the Town Council will give us the deeds to the strip mall and the ranch house free and clear. I already have a construction company that will rebuild the entire mall for less than the price we can sell our home for."

"NO, NO, NO! I will not live here," said Melissa.

"What if you could have your very own business? It would be right next door to the bakery. And I promise I will keep Natee from marrying anyone until she is well into her thirties," said Howard.

Melissa stood there for a long while stone dead quiet. "What kind of business?" she finally asked.

"Whatever kind of business you want. Take a drive around the whole town and look for what they don't have," said Howard.

"Okay, I'll give it one year. If I don't like it after that we are leaving. And I'll still hold you to your promise of Natee not getting married until she is over thirty," said Melissa.

Their discussion was interrupted by a knock on their bedroom door. Howard opened the door with Natee standing there.

"There is a big celebration going on in the whole town. Is it okay if I go with my boyfriend Wesley to the celebration?"

"Yes of course, Natee. But be home for dinner. We have plans and projects to talk about," said Howard.

Natee went scurrying out the front door and grabbed Wesley's hand.

"Oh that was good. That will keep her from getting married before she is thirty. Edna Brown may be right about one thing, we are in the elite class of knowing who are and who aren't."

Howard didn't ask the question that was on his mind. "Who are and aren't what?"

They were interrupted again, this time by Fitzpatrick and Donavan. "We met twin sisters last night, Gwendolyn and Elphaba. They want to take us to this town celebration.

After hearing the girl's names, Melissa sat down on the bed and began to cry.

Chapter Twenty Two
The Wizard Bank

When Broomstick got back to normal, relatively speaking, and everyone was back to work. Winston contacted the Keystone's to make them a formal offer of the strip mall and ranch house properties.

The meeting took place in Mayor Winston's office at City Hall. "I can safely speak for the entire community of Broomstick when I say, we want your family to live here and open the bakery," said Winston.

"I do not understand why this bakery is so important. I have driven all over this town and there are plenty of bakeries throughout," said Melissa.

"I see you don't understand the location. It would be near the cemetery," said Winston.

Howard commented, "Someone said to me at Natee's party that they missed the smell of fresh baked bread and pastries early in the morning just before sunrise."

"That is exactly my point, Mr. Keystone," said Winston. "There has always been a bakery there and the cemetery will attract customers. You haven't grasped the concept that we use the cemetery as a place to celebrate. We enjoy a good dead man's party and people will stop in to buy your baked goods just to take them to the cemetery for a picnic with their departed loved ones."

Melissa whispered something in Howard's ear. Howard then asked, "Do you drink wine and eat cheese at these parties?"

"Mrs. Keystone, we eat and drink all the same things just like anyone else. Having magical abilities really doesn't make us different," said Winston.

Winston passed over a formal printed document with language that only a lawyer could possible understand after hours of running a fine tooth comb through it. Howard and Melissa sat there trying to read it.

"Mr. and Mrs. Keystone, this is your world document that the township lawyers have made up. Let me tell you what it says in my world. You will receive both deeds to the strip mall and the ranch house properties free and clear. You have to of course pay any taxes owed. You have one year to rebuild the entire mall or the property reverts back to Broomstick," said Winston.

"That sounds too good to be true," said Melissa. "If it is that simple, then why such a large document?"

"Because of the other things I haven't told you about. With this I will grant college scholarships to your sons and employment after completion of their bachelor degrees, if and only if you allow us to educate your daughter with our disciplines without any interference.

"What you mean to say, we get all this for free in return for our daughter," said Melissa.

"It's really not quite as harsh as you make it, Mrs. Keystone. I'm offering the best education for all three of your children. Natee just needs specialized tutoring that you can't give her.

Howard asked, "Does this contract need to be signed in blood?"

"No Mr. Keystone, you may use your own pen if that will make you feel better," said Winston.

Natee was called into Winston's office after her parents had signed the contract and received the title deeds that the Olsen's had given to Broomstick over a year ago.

"Natee we have some unfinished business that we started when we were in the medical ward together," said Winston. "Let me show you around town and we'll discuss a plan."

Over in the magical broom production building Natee was shown the assembly line. "Oh I remember them. They did my hair, makeup, and clothes for the witch's coven," said Natee as she waved at the nymphs. They smiled and waved back at her.

Winston led Natee into Franklin's personal library. Hawkins was there holding the door open. "Welcome Mr. Wisestone, gud ta see ya again," said Hawkins. "Hello missy, if'n you need a baby sitter…"

"Hawkins, let's leave it at hello missy," said Agnes.

Franklin, Harriet, Peter, and Agnes were sitting around a stone table when Natee came in the room. The bottle was sitting in the middle of the table. Up against the back wall sat three other men Natee only recognized as the wizards that were with Winston when the accident happened.

"Have a chair, Natee," said Winston. "Now tell me about what you discovered in the Realm of Forbidden Magic."

"I didn't discover it because it was given to me," said Natee. She pulled out of her pocket the paper that Euphoria had given her. "This is the directions to the portal to the Outside of the Universe. I think Euphoria wanted to, you know, just leave and never come back."

"You said to me that you think this would be a good place to dispose of this bottle," said Winston. "Can I see that paper you have there?"

"I could, but that would change the location of the portal. I have to take you to where it is at. Then it will change again and the knowledge of it whereabouts will be back in the Realm of Forbidden Magic," said Natee.

"I guess there is no reason to argue about it then. You have already accepted the dangers involved," said Winston. "Can you at least give us a hint?"

"No, but I need to learn how to go places on my own, like to the Wizard's Bank," said Natee.

"And so you shall," said Franklin. "Peter, would you tutor Natee on this matter? And when you are ready Natee we will go on your adventure together."

Peter taught Natee various ways of leaving and entering places. He started with the basics. "Do you know why Harry Houdini failed in getting out of his water torture cell?"

"Because he didn't have magical powers?" said Natee.

"No, he had limited magical powers. I was once like Houdini. I had limited magical powers and I couldn't transport myself out of a wet paper bag," said Peter.

"He and I were trying to move too much stuff. The trick to magical transportation, some even call it transindigitation, is to limit moving just you and not the surrounding air or water as in Houdini's case."

Peter had Natee walk from one room to another, and then to the outside. "That's it slide between here and there. You see if you tried that with water surrounding you it wouldn't fit through. Okay that's enough for today we'll work on distances tomorrow."

Natee asked, "What about The Wizard's Bank?"

"I'll take you there right now. Stand next to me and we'll go together," said Peter.

Peter whistled and pushed on the air in front of him. The door opened and Natee followed Peter into the bank. It was a large marbled place with a W etched in the floor with two crossed wands over it.

Peter and Natee walked over to the desk that had the sign 'New Accounts' hanging above it. On the desk was a name plate. 'Mr. Wishenwel'.

"May I help you?" said Mr. Wishenwel.

"Miss Keystone would like to open an account," said Peter.

He pulled out a few forms that needed to be filled out by Natee.

She scanned down the first form. "What does this mean, Peter?" asked Natee.

"Just put no in that box," said Peter.

"But what does it mean?" Natee asked again.

"Natee I would say ask your parents, but maybe it would be better if you asked Agnes or Harriet. Just put no," said Peter.

"Do you want to make this a wand account? We have a special this century of earning magic credits toward a purchase of a time share, where you can share the same time with a departed relative," said Mr. Wishenwel.

"No, just a regular account for Miss Keystone," said Peter.

Peter whispered, "They take the time off at the end of your life to actually pay for it."

"And how much do you wish to deposit?" asked Mr. Wishenwel.

Natee set the bag of gold coins on the desk. Mr. Wishenwel looked inside the bag at the gold coins. He removed one coin and examined it.

He put the coin back in the bag and with a disgruntled expression. We haven't minted those wizens in some time.'

Mr. Wishenwel handed all the paperwork to Natee and said, "Window number nine for gold purity and weight."

Peter and Natee stood in the line at window number nine for nearly ten minutes. "These wizens are pretty old. They are heavier than today's wizens," said Peter while passing the time.

Natee stepped up to the window and handed all the paperwork to the ogre with a smile. Then she put one of her old wizen gold coins on the counter.

The ogre picked up the coin and held it up to his eye. "Oh I'm sorry I can't help you," said the ogre at window number nine. "The Bank Manager's door is at the end of the hall."

The ogre handed the paperwork back to Natee. The ogre attempted to close his window. Peter put his magic wand in the way.

"The wizen if you please," said Peter.

The ogre handed a new wizen to Peter.

"Nooo...The wizen the little lady handed you for examination," stated Peter while jabbing his wand in at the ogre.

The ogre slid the old wizen to Peter. Peter handed the new wizen back to the ogre.

Peter and Natee walked to the Bank Manager's door. Just inside the door was a receptionist. On the desk was a wood routed nameplate. Peter had seen the nameplate before and the person that it belonged to.

"Miss Patty Whack," said Peter.

"Mr. Candlewick what do I owe the pleasure," said Miss Patty Whack.

"Natee here is trying to open an account," said Peter.

Miss Patty Whack the receptionist to the Bank Manager's office looked at the forms and said, "You need to go to window number nine."

Peter explained, "We already stood in that line for ten minutes just to be sent here to see the Bank Manager by a thieving ogre that tried to steel one of Natee's old wizen coins."

Peter handed the old wizen to Miss Patty Whack. Miss Patty Whack stood up and looked down at window number nine. "I see the problem. It's one of those underworld ogres here for training."

About that time the Bank Manager came out of his office with some paperwork for Miss Patty Whack. That is when he spied the coin sitting on the desk. He picked the gold coin up and twiddled the coin about his fingers.

"Where did you get this gold coin?" asked the Bank Manager.

Natee said, "Out of my bag I got from the Realm of Forbidden Magic."

"Come into my office and we'll take care of this little matter for you," said the Bank Manager.

The Bank Manager flipped the coin to Miss Patty Whack. She caught it with her index finger and thumb.

"Have it weighed and purity check. You know window number nine," said the Bank Manger as he closed the door.

The Bank Manager thumbed through a book until he found a picture of the coin. "Yes here it is. The exchange rate is…" he passed his finger down a column and stopped on a figure. "How many do you have in this bag?"

"Thirty nine hundred," said Natee.

"It may take us a while. In the mean time here is your deposit slip stating the number of coins until we calculate the exact exchange rate of these rare coins."

Peter and Natee sat outside of the Bank Manager's office while many people walked in and out of the office. Finally he called them back in. James Candlewick was standing there next to the desk where stacks of thirty nine hundred coins were evenly laid out. Next to the stacks of old coins was a couple of stacks of new freshly minted new wizens. The bag seemed to be filled with new gold coins.

"I don't understand it. We counted out thirty nine hundred coins from the bag and the bag started to have new normal wizens. It is still full," said the Bank Manager.

"Natee how much money do you think you'll need for your lifetime?" asked James. "Would ten million be enough?"

"I, uh, I guess so," said Natee.

James turned to the bank manager and said, "Put ten million wizens in her account. Keep the thirty nine out of the bag for sale to collectors to raise the ten million wizens plus commission. Seal the bag and put it in a deposit vault under Miss Keystone's name. If for some reason she needs more money, take out the required number of new coins from the bag and reseal it."

"Natee not only did you get some rare gold coins, you also received the even rarer unicorn messenger bag. The bag can never be emptied," said James. "And it now officially belongs to you."

"I'm rich? I mean I'm really rich? I can buy anything I want? Oh I want to start by giving a million whatever's to my dad to build his bakery. And, and a million to a good charity. This is going to be so much fun," said Natee.

"We'll have a custodian appointed to you until you are older," said James. "Peter, you are now the custodian of her account. Take care of her needs."

Peter and Natee returned back to his house where Wesley had been waiting for Natee. "We'll find a good charity and I'm sure the money for your dad's bakery is already in the works,"

"Peter, can I go shopping?" asked Natee.

Katee and Natee went uptown to the knotem part of town where the Düben outlet store was located. Katee would suggest and Natee would try on all sorts of looks and designs. Natee went for quiet let me blend in styles.

Down the street was a camping and wilderness sports store where Natee got excited about buying clothes.

Natee stood in the hunting clothes area of the store. "Yes this jungle camouflage outfit with rugged hiking boots. Where can I try it on? Oh, I need wool socks. The thin synthetic breathable ones please."

It was a very dense and muggy jungle that Natee had brought them all to. Insects were swarming around their heads and things crawled on the ground across their feet if they stop walking.

"Follow me, it's this way," said Natee in her jungle camouflage outfit with rugged hiking boots with Wesley dressed the same right behind her.

Agnes and Franklin were not too far behind when Agnes tripped over a tree root that was sticking out of the ground. Franklin caught Agnes by her arm before she fell flat on her face.

Franklin stopped just for a moment to view some of the floral. "I must pick some of these to study what it could possible do."

Winston, Peter and the other three wizards took turns carrying the heavy bottle of dingy water with the emotions of Jack the Ripper trapped inside.

Natee stopped in front of an ancient carved rock that was covered by a giant spider web. "Where is the spider?" asked Wesley.

It didn't take long for his question to be answered when a sticky silk rope wrapped around him and was beginning to pull him up.

Natee didn't have time to pull out her wand. She pointed her fingers at the spider that was hanging above them in the tree branches. She made a move like she was using a knife and cut the silk rope. Wesley fell just a couple of feet and rolled on the ground. Dead leaves and twigs stuck to the sticky rope.

The spider scurried back into its hiding place. Soon thereafter thick ooze was seen accumulating where the spider was.

Agnes could see Natee's eyes. They turned all black for that short moment.

Franklin used his magic to remove the silk rope from Wesley and helped him up.

Natee used a dead tree branch to move the spider web from the carved rock to expose the rusty riveted metal doors with four symbols.

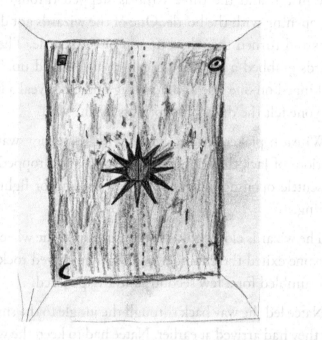

From her pocket she pulled out the paper that Euphoria had given her. Natee pushed on the symbols in the order that were on the paper. First she pushed the crescent moon. Next was the circle with a dot in the middle.

"Do you see a square within a square with a solid rectangle in the center?" asked Natee.

"There up in the left hand corner," said Wesley.

Natee found it and pushed the square symbol. In the center of the two doors was either a spider or a symbol of the sun, Natee wasn't sure, but she pushed the symbol.

The two doors moved in two directions from the center like sliding glass doors. It revealed a chamber with an iron scuttle in the floor.

"This is it," said Natee.

Winston and the three wizards stepped through the carved rock opening with the bottle. One of the wizards got down on his knees and turned the wheel on top of the scuttle. The other two wizards grabbed a hold of the wheel and pulled up. The scuttle was hinged on one side and it swung open to reveal a black abyss. Everyone felt the draw of emptiness by the void.

Winston picked up the bottle with the dingy water and the emotions of Jack the Ripper sealed inside and dropped it through the scuttle opening. There wasn't any sound or light flash, just nothing.

The wizards closed the scuttle and turned the wheel to close it. Everyone exited the chamber quietly. The carved rock slid closed then rumbled for a few seconds and disappeared.

Natee led the way back through the jungle to the small clearing that they had arrived at earlier. Natee had to keep the whereabouts of this portal secret or it would change.

"It's time we went to the Poison Apple Tavern and celebrated," said Winston.

Winston and the three wizards first toasted each other for finishing what they had started together with mugs of ale. They clang them together and drank until the mugs were empty. After that it was an evening of food and merriment for the group.

Wesley asked Natee, "Have you ever had rich foamy carbonated witch hazelnut soda?"

"No, I never even heard of it," said Natee. But when she took a drink of it, her eyes opened wide. "Yes I have had this before. When I was in the realm I conjured up a pizza and this came with it."

Agnes and Franklin sent the two children home after they had eaten. "Your parent's said that both of you need to be ready for school tomorrow."

"Witchcraft school?" asked Natee.

"No not witchcraft school, the regular knotem junior high school that the other children attend. Your parents insisted that you still go to school," said Agnes.

"My mom insists that I go too. She says it is good for me to learn to co-exist with nonmagical people my own age," said Wesley.

At the crossroad between their homes, Wesley said, "I'll see you tomorrow at the bus stop in the morning."

"The bus stop? Can't we just show up at the school yard?" asked Natee.

"Mom says no magic at school no matter what," said Wesley.

"I'm not so sure I can do that, but we'll see," said Natee.

It was the first day of school. For Natee that meant, first time in Junior high school, a new school, and not knowing anyone. "Yeah, no magic, let the first stuck up rich girl try to rub my face in makeup and we'll see about not using magic," said Natee wearing her drab blend in clothes.

Natee also found out that she and Wesley wouldn't have any classes together because she is in the seventh grade and Wesley was in the eighth grade.

"You never told me you were a year older than me," said Natee at lunch.

"I'm only thirteen, but I skipped a grade," answered Wesley. "I can help you with your homework. I kept all the homework assignments from last year."

After lunch Natee was in the locker room for gym class. A group of three girls were eyeing her from across the room.

"Hey you, you're new here," said one of the girls.

Natee looked down the locker row. "Yeah, I'm new here." and went back to putting on her gym shoes.

They started to walk toward her. In one of the girl's hand was a makeup compact. Natee stood up and faced them. "You girls like putting on makeup?"

Natee flashed her two fingers at the three girls and gave them a complete makeover of striped hair, red eye shadow accented with white and black lines that curled around their temples, and blue lipstick on and around their mouths. She changed their clothes into tube tops and ragged denim miniskirts.

When gym class was over she saw the girls were still trying to wash off the makeup and hair color. It was just a little faded.

After school Natee was waiting at the bus stop for Wesley when the three girls came up to her. They still had the crazy makeup and hair. "You're going to pay for this," said one of the girls.

"I think you three need a lesson in manners," said Natee.

Natee pulled out her magic wand and held it up to her eyes and said, "Time plus five."

Natee and the three girls disappeared for about five minutes. When they reappeared at the bus stop Natee was standing there quiet ignoring the three girls.

Wesley walked out of the schoolyard up to Natee. Wesley looked at the three girls with normal hair and makeup and bland clothing. They were standing there holding their notebooks waiting for the bus.

Wesley gestured toward the bus door to the three girls. They quietly went to the back of the bus. Natee and Wesley sat in front. The doors shut and the bus drove off.

"Did you do something?" asked Wesley.

"Do what?" asked Natee.

"Nothing," said Wesley.

205

Chapter Twenty Three
Who has The Power

Howard was doing well with the 'Keystone's Bakery'. He had designer cakes for Friday the thirteenth, March twenty ninth Smoke and Mirrors Day, October first Magic Circle Day. Of course he had the traditional holidays of Halloween, Occult Day, and the big one, Summer Solstice.

Natee would complain about some of his ideas to sell bakery goods. "Da-ad, these are not glazed crystal balls, they're donut holes. And those are churros, not powder sugar covered magic wands."

His big sales were his old world breads. They went well with the wares sold next door, 'Melissa's House of Imported Cheeses and Wines'.

Melissa was semi happy. She had her own business that had no real competition. People were stocking up on imported wines for their cellars.

It was still the magical world that annoyed her. Witches and wizards would just show up unannounced in her store. They didn't use the front door much. Money was a big problem. "How much is a wizen, and what bank in Broomstick accepts them as currency?" asked Melissa to Howard.

Melissa was even more annoyed that her sons married those twin witches, Gwendolyn and Elphaba. They were in Melissa's face constantly about something or another. Because of them, Natee was left alone to do whatever she did as a witch. She came and went as she pleased.

Natee learned her magic from the Sisters of the Q. She leaned more toward the magical style of Mary Pride one of the founding sisters. Mary was very helpful, but cautioned Natee on some of the techniques that she was using.

Mary said to Agnes one day, "Watch Natee closely, her methods tend to be even darker than I would do. Her white magic is still dominating."

Wesley even noticed that Natee seemed to have a lingering shade of dark mist in her eyes after some of her spells were done. "Sometimes you scare me, Natee, with your magic."

Natee kissed Wesley and said, "Don't worry I'm not going to hex you."

When Natee was the age of sixteen, her brothers were both married to the twin girls. Fitzpatrick was married to Gwendolyn and Donavan married Elphaba. It wasn't exactly a happy relationship between the sister in laws and Natee.

Elphaba said in front of Natee to Donavan, "It's really too bad that your family had that tragedy that left you with a sorceress for a sister."

Natee turned with darken eyes at Elphaba. "I like being a

sorceress. And thank you for recognizing that I am more powerful then you and your sister put together. But really, we should be a lot nicer to each other. That is what my Great Great Grandmother Shasta would want us to do."

Natee was stumped about two writings of the same reincarnation spell. There was the one written in Shasta's shadow book. "Ference Eso Dabblo Zate"

And there was Euphoria spell. "Ference Gusto en Debblas Zate."

Natee kept going back and forth from Shasta's shadow book to her shadow book that she wrote while in the medical ward.

"This one was changed in Shasta's shadow book. The change is in Mukul's handwriting. Why?"

Natee's eyes opened wide. "Why? To bring him back from the dead after his amulet was pieced back together. And I know now what Euphoria was up to and why she wanted me killed at the opening of the tunnel. Euphoria wanted my pure black amulet to help her do this reincarnation spell to bring herself back!"

Natee figured out how Euphoria wanted Mukul to free her from her captivity. "This finally all makes sense," said Natee.

Over the three years since Mukul had died. Natee became a little older and a lot smarter.

While she was in the marbled building on the Island of Truth in the Realm of Forbidden Magic she went around to all the rooms listening to spells and potions and learning magical knowledge that had been lost through time.

Over the years Natee had wondered about things that Mukul had said. "The timing of what he had said was all wrong."

Natee thought, "He said, 'I had the keys to unlock the jail all along and didn't even know I had them.' What was he referring to?"

Natee had another thought, "When he held out his hand and placed the orange amulet in it, the one shard emerged from the scar in his hand and joined with the amulet. Mukul's spider scar disappeared. Time had caught up with him also as with Euphoria. They both died at the same time."

This occurred to Natee, "He said, 'My pure hearted act is to retrieve the one that has always loved me.' Mukul wasn't talking first person. Those were the words for me to say. I had the keys to unlock the jail all along and didn't even know I had them. My pure hearted act is to retrieve the one that has always loved me."

Natee knew now what she had to do. "I have to go back to the Realm of Forbidden Magic and get Mukul. That is what this whole thing was all about. And Mukul knew that it would no longer be a curse, but be a part of the amulet's power for immortality," said Natee.

Natee retrieved Shasta's cauldron and Mukul's staff. She stood out under the full moonlight and holding up the staff with the globe on top held by carved dragon talons and chanted, "Pure as white even in night. I sing the song of the Unicorn Pond."

Natee walked through the light and out onto the sandy rocky land just before the oasis where the Unicorn Reflection Pond was. Near the edge of the pond she found the two piles of ashen remains and Shasta's black protection cape. She sat down the cauldron next to them.

Natee picked up Shasta's cape and put it in her bag.

Natee guessed that the one closer to the entrance was Euphoria.

She gently put her fingers in the ash and pulled out Euphoria' dark green amulet and blew off any remaining ash. Natee didn't see the two orange shards within the ashes.

Natee wrapped the amulet in a handkerchief and put it in her pocket. Then she paid careful attention to the other pile of ashes. She scooped up the remains and placed them in the cauldron. Natee was very careful to get all of it.

She noticed in the middle of the pile with Mukul's orange amulet was a rock with a blood stain on it.

"Strange, that he dripped blood on a rock. Or maybe I needed more of him than just ashes."

She left the blood stained rock in the cauldron with the orange amulet and the ashes. From the Unicorn Reflection Pond she filled a potion bottle with water and put it in her other pocket

Natee was just about to leave with the cauldron filled with Mukul's ashes when she turned and kicked Euphoria's ashes into the clear water of the pond. The water fizzed with black smoke as the ashes sank to the bottom.

Natee then said with a charitable forgiving merciful voice of Shasta coming from her white magical side, "I told you I was a very powerful witch."

Natee waited for the night of new moon when the sky and magic were at their darkest hour. She flew on her broom with many detours and stealth maneuvers through clouds to ensure she wasn't followed out to her secluded desert hideaway.

She began to prepare a witches circle of magic. Natee carefully sweep the ground clear of anything dead, like insects, plant twigs and leaves, and animal remains.

The cauldron with Mukul's ashes was placed in the center of the swept area. Natee opened her bag and pulled out the black hooded cape. She twirled the cape open slid her arms through the wide sleeves and pulled the hood over her head.

Natee held her staff in her left hand. With the blunt end of the staff Natee drew the protective witch's circle around her and the cauldron.

Natee began to follow the spell that she had studied relentlessly to ensure she would do it correctly. She filled in the etched magic circle with sand from an hourglass by breaking one end of the glass and slowly walking the circle pouring the sand out.

When all was set and the hour was approaching midnight, Natee placed the end of the staff in the cauldron and down into the ashes with the orange amulet and the blood stained rock. She held the staff straight up and chanted, "Ference Eso Dabblo Zate. Reverse this one's fate. REINCARNATE!"

The ashes churned and bubbled. Black sooty smoke began to rise out of the cauldron and started to take shape of a man holding the staff with both hands opposite of Natee.

Mukul smiled at Natee. "Hello my dear Natee. Shasta was right. You were the right choice to do the pure hearted act."

Natee let go of the staff and hugged Mukul tightly. She hid her face in his shoulder to keep him from seeing her cry. "I would do it all over again for you Grandfather," said Natee.

"Let's go and get something to eat," said Mukul.

Natee swept the circle away and sent the cauldron and the broom home. With Mukul's arm around her shoulder they disappeared into the night arriving at the entrance to the Bombay Palace Restaurant.

Mukul and Natee were sitting at a round table in the lavish Bombay Palace Restaurant dining on an assortment platter of pakoras, samosa, chicken tikka, and seeekh kababs.

Natee was admiring the surroundings. Hanging in the middle of the dining area was a three-tiered Czech crystal chandelier. Portraits of royal personages and brass fixtures, imported from Muradabad lined the walls. The floor was covered with plush Scottish wool carpeting. "I could get use to living like this," said Natee.

"And you should," said Mukul. "You're rich enough to afford to live in a palace decorated like this. Oh, I have something for you."

Mukul handed Natee a black velvet box. Natee opened it to find inside a neckless. Hanging from it was a single golden eye with a flame for the iris.

"Oh it is so beautiful. What does the symbol mean?" asked Natee.

"It stands for royal power, good health, and above all protection," answered Mukul.

Natee clasped the neckless around her neck feeling very powerful. "I will always wear it."

Neither had seen the man approaching from behind them and possibly for a good reason.

"Mind if I join you for a bite of lunch?" asked James Candlewick.

Natee choked on some of her food, but recovered quickly by drinking down some water. Mukul sat there peacefully not showing any signs of surprise.

"Please be our guest. I recommend the Lamb Chops Kandhari," said Mukul.

James spoke softly to the waiter and then turned back to Mukul and Natee.

Natee stopped eating as her face was flushed and at a loss of words. She knew without asking why James was there.

Natee dreadfully thought, "He's going to accuse me of being an evil sorceress or worse, a black magic necromanceress."

"I see you made it back from your journey to Nirvana in one piece," said James, as if Mukul had just been on a pleasure trip. "Did you have a good rest?"

"Oh I did indeed, thank you for asking," said Mukul.

"That was a bit of real dark magic for such a young witch. I might even go as far as saying black necromancy should have been way out of your league at your age," said James looking directly at Natee.

Natee felt the icy cold stare of James down to her bones. He was without a doubt angry.

The waiter came and sat a bowl of Mulligtawny soup and a basket of paratha stuffed with mint in front of James.

"I don't believe we have broken any magical laws," said Mukul while continuing to eat.

Natee sat quietly wishing she could just leave. Then she said, "I need to go to the ladies room." Out of politeness both men stood up while Natee left the table.

Natee found an empty stall and fell to her knees. She vomited till she couldn't spit up anymore. She was sickened by the feelings she received from James.

After Natee cleaned herself up, she looked in the mirror at her reflection. "I am stronger and more powerful than he is. I won't ever let him do this to me again. My white power is supreme."

Natee's eyes showed a hint of gray where the whites of her eyes should have been just before her eyes turned completely black then back to white. Mukul felt a dreadful twinge within him.

James continued the conversation with Mukul after Natee had left. "No you didn't break any magical laws, but you are influencing Natee with dark magic that no one should be doing. You should have stayed dead, Mukul. This is too dangerous of magic to be doing, especially with a young witch."

Natee caught her composure and returned to the table. She gestured to the waiter to take her plate away.

James turned his attention to Natee and asked, "Do you love Wesley?"

Natee stared at James wondering what does this have to do with bringing Mukul back from the dead. "I guess so, I'm not sure I would be using the word love. I like him very much." Then she turned defensive, "I'm only sixteen we are not old enough to be thinking about love."

"I can't see your future because your magic won't allow it. I can see, however, Wesley's. At your thirteenth birthday party, you stole his heart. When the time comes, he can love no one but you," said James. "If you're old enough to do necromancy, you are old enough to crush a boy's soul."

Natee sat at the table thinking back to her thirteenth birthday party. *"I didn't..., yes I did. I remember. It was when I saw my reflection in his eyes. I felt my magical powers surge for a moment and then I smiled at Wesley. It was soon after that he asked me to be his girlfriend. I thought I already was, but it was I that had said that he was my boyfriend. I didn't ask and I just took Wesley for granted."*

James wiped his mouth with a cloth napkin and really showed Natee some attention. "It was your black magic that stole his heart for your white magic side. I'm not saying it was wrong. I'm saying you have to be aware of its power. The white amulet you received didn't suppress your black magic, they joined forces with it. And now you are being influenced to do magic darker than I think you realize."

Mukul started to say something, but James put up his hand and continued to talk to Natee. "Wesley is my family, and someday you will also be a part of the Candlewick's. Don't ruin your life along with Wesley's with this direction you are being led."

"Can I answer your question again, Mr. Candlewick?" asked Natee.

"I already know the answer, Natee. That is why I'm here, to keep the answer from changing," said James.

Chapter Twenty Four
Truth and lies

At age eighteen and finally graduated from knotem high school Natee disappeared without a trace.

Natee ran off with Mukul to live a secluded life far away from other's influences, namely James Candlewick.

"I'm not ready to marry Wesley Candlewick yet. James Candlewick thought my answer was yes when I wanted to tell him the answer was no."

Well hidden in the Asian jungle of Cambodia was a hut that blended in with the surroundings. Mukul sat on the floor sipping tea with Natee on that first night.

"I must tell you my secret and abolish all lies," said Mukul.

"I don't want to hear it. It doesn't matter anymore. I set you free," stated Natee.

"It isn't over. There is still more work to do and I need your help. If you don't hear the truth than everything I have done will be for nothing," said Mukul as he sipped his tea.

"I will help no matter what, Grandfather. It doesn't matter what you have said or done to get this far," said Natee.

"After I tell you this you may not want to help me anymore, but it must be told. Now sit and listen please," said Mukul.

"My plan was to hide my soul on the Outside of the Universe and substitute another's in my place. It was simple and brilliant, death would be deceived by the substitution and I would merely reclaim my own soul back from the Outside of the Universe and live forever. I would have slipped right through the fingers of death," began Mukul.

"My plan was interrupted by Tanaka Drake. Someone informed him of my situation of healing that little girl. I learned later it was Euphoria. She wanted in on my plan to deceive death. I told her that this plan would work only once," stated Mukul.

"She got angry with me and planted the seed of conspiracy to grow into a witch's council," said Mukul.

"I thought she loved you? Why would she do this to you?" asked Natee.

"Euphoria stopped the execution and caused me to be cursed for eternity. She knew about the curse of the spider spell. This was her way of giving me immortality to allow me to use that little girl's soul for her," explained Mukul.

"I told her of another way. It would take three souls to complete the magical math of immortality, one to lead, one to follow, and one to be left alone," said Mukul.

"That would have been you, Euphoria, and the girl's soul. Am I right?" said Natee.

"Yes you are right, except..." Mukul paused for a moment.

"Except the curse stood in the way," finished Natee.

"That was the death card to the whole plan. I still needed a pure hearted act to remove the curse," said Mukul showing a little temper.

"I needed Euphoria to go to the Realm of Forbidden Magic to retrieve my amulet fragments. Unknown to me was her scheme that would include retrieving something else from the Outside of the Universe," added Mukul.

"After years of waiting for her to return, I knew that she had failed and was killed by the creatures that guard the entrance to the realm. As it turned out she spent a century in the realm collecting all the tiny fragments of my amulet. She could never leave the Realm of Forbidden Magic because real time was waiting just outside to claim her years of life," explained Mukul.

"I was told that after being there a week I was malnourished and dehydrated even though I ate and drank in the realm." stated Natee.

Mukul got up and refilled his cup with fresh hot tea. He stood by an open air window looking out at the jungle.

"As I lived my secluded life on top of that mountain overlooking the valley in my small wooden shack that my feeble magic could make, I was visited by what I thought was the ghost of Euphoria. It turned out that she was still alive and had indeed collected all the fragments of my amulet. She learned to project herself from the realm."

"Euphoria said to me, Mukul get me the Hourglass of the Time Bandits that lies hidden in the caves within the portal to the Outside of the Universe. I can use it to reverse time."

Mukul turned around to face Natee and sipped his tea. "The Hourglass of the Time Bandits was a magical myth, I told her."

"There are magical myths?" asked Natee.

Mukul really didn't answer Natee's question directly. "She insisted that it was real. I went to the place where the portal was. It had vanished. We both figured out that no two persons could know where it was located. Thus was the dilemma. She knew the whereabouts of the portal but could not tell me. She grew angry with me as I would not send someone in just to get the information."

"The day I met Shasta was the luckiest day of my tortured life. I had gone to a town where I had never been before to get some potion supplies. She was there buying healing supplies. Perfect I thought to myself," said Mukul.

"You were going to send her to the Realm of Forbidden Magic?" ask Natee.

"Not for the information of the portal to the Outside of the Universe," said Mukul. "I needed my amulet to do anything that would remotely be involved in going there."

"So what stopped you from sending Grandma Shasta?" asked Natee.

"I learned that Shasta was married to a man that wasn't a wizard. We continued a plutonic relationship with magic being our connection," stated Mukul. "Euphoria soon found about Shasta. She became angry when I wouldn't send her to get the location of the portal."

"Shasta did a spell while the child was in the womb to ensure magic would be passed along. She bore a child, a girl she named Gertrud."

"My grandmother."

"Yes Melissa's mother hadn't any magic to pass on. I figured it was because of her husband not being a wizard. I later found out that Euphoria came to her as a voice and told her a bad spell. It was a cloaking spell," told Mukul.

"Was it this spell? "I read this spell and saw the spell didn't fit the title to the words of the spell," asked Natee as she held open Shasta's shadow book.

Mukul hung his head. "Yes that is the spell. Euphoria caused Shasta to cancel out her magic. It was Euphoria that stopped the magic from being passed to Gertrud."

"I knew it. She was very angry that I had very strong black magical powers when I shouldn't have had any at all," said Natee.

"I resolved to help Shasta with passing down her magical powers to an heir. We, together performed a magical spell that bonded us together. Later in years, to our surprise, you showed an aura of magic," stated Mukul.

"You stirred up the lost family magic?" asked Natee.

"Partly, yes. Shasta was quite old by this time and her husband had passed on years ago…" Mukul started to say.

"You…You…You're my…" Natee just couldn't bring her to say what she was thinking.

"I was able to collect a large locket of Shasta's hair. I made a potion with it and skin flakes from me. The spell I used collected only the black magic of Shasta's amulet leaving her with only a pure white amulet. I asked Shasta to invite Melissa over for some tea," Mukul relented.

"Shasta, I said to her later that night. I have a dark secret to tell you. I have given you an heir. Your new granddaughter has your magic," explained Mukul.

"My parents aren't my parents. Shasta is my…" Natee sat there in complete disbelief shaking her head. "And you…"

"No, no, you don't understand the magic. I reconciled the wrong that Euphoria had done. Shasta and I are just the progenitorship of your magical power. We woke it up," explained Mukul.

Natee got up and walked over to the open air window and stared out at the jungle. Tears slowly formed in her eyes. Uncertainty of what to think set in.

"You would grow up under my care and training. At the right age I would have you enter the Realm of Forbidden Magic and retrieve my amulet and the location of the portal to the Outside of the Universe from Euphoria," said Mukul wondering what Natee was thinking.

Natee turned around and faced Mukul with a harden face. "Alright, I get it. I did what you wanted, all of it. Now what?"

"I was set with everything. I had my amulet and Euphoria had the spell to deceive the Grim Reaper himself. It takes three souls to complete the magical math of immortality, one to lead, one to follow, and one to be left alone," said Mukul.

"So you completed the spell. Euphoria and the girl are with you also? I brought back to life all three of you and now you have your precious immortality," said Natee with distaste.

Mukul continued, "I didn't do the spell. Euphoria and the girl's soul are in Nirvana."

"Stop it! Just stop. I heard enough," screamed Natee with complete blackness in her eyes.

"I picked up the rock with your blood on it hoping you would reincarnate me with it in my ashes. I didn't forgive Euphoria for trying to kill you. She would have been very dangerous to just leave her as the one to be alone in the Realm of Forbidden Magic. I had to eliminate her once and for all," continued Mukul without looking at Natee.

"I don't have immortality. Because of your blood on the rock, we are attached to each other," said Mukul.

"And that makes only two," said Natee.

Mukul sat down on the floor and sipped his cold tea. Natee just stood there staring at him wondering whether to hate him or pity him.

"So do you have the Hourglass of the Time Bandits?" ask Natee.

"I can't get it alone. I tried to tell Euphoria that," said Mukul.

"Then what are we waiting for? Let's go and get it," said Natee as she changed her attitude.

Natee took Mukul to the door without him knowing where it was so the location would not change. It took many trips over a few years to locate the hourglass.

Natee was a couple months away from her twenty fourth birthday. Mukul had aged also, which was something he hadn't done in a very long time.

"There it is over on that landing," squawked Mukul.

They held onto the rock face and slid their feet along the ledge. At the end was a small landing, just big enough for one person.

Mukul tried to get on the landing. He slipped off the ledge just before the landing where the hourglass was lying. He barely got a grab onto the ledge with his hands. He knew that he couldn't hold on much longer.

"The one that possesses the hourglass controls his or her time, death cannot touch their souls. I want you to make a promise to Wesley with your fingers crossed. Promise to love him for all eternity. Now go and have a long life with Wesley. He deserves to be loved by you more than I do." Mukul smiled at Natee and let go of the ledge.

Chapter Twenty Five
Sands through the Hourglass

Wesley went on with his life trying not to think of Natee. He went to the College of Pseudo Science and Metaphysics to study magical technology.

From time to time Natee would show up at his door exhausted and hungry. Sometimes she showed up lying on the porch needing medical attention. Natee never would tell him where she had been or what she was doing.

At age twenty three Wesley was a magical engineer. He had his own business that designed and made magic wands that used a precision cultured spun Stiltskin wire wrapped synthetic ruby crystal to amplify one's magic. It had a faster sleeker beam of magic.

He loved Natee very much. He had thoughts of marrying her and starting a family of little Candlewicks. He just couldn't live with her disappearing and showing up months later without any explanations.

Natee showed up on her twenty fourth birthday at Wesley's front door. She was filthy from head to toe. Her clothes were ragged and hardly covering her body. She had sticky spider silk rope pieces stuck to her back. Next to her was a large burlap sack tied shut with the same sticky silk rope. Natee whispered with a dry throat, "I did it." Then she passed out.

When Natee awoke, she was in the magical medical ward of the Broomstick Hospital. Sitting in a chair next to her bed was Wesley. In front of him on the floor was the burlap sack still tied shut.

"Wesley?" said Natee.

Wesley stirred and opened his eyes and looked at Natee.

"Wesley?" said Natee. "Do you love me?"

"Yes Natee I love you. I have loved you since that first night you kissed me," said Wesley.

"I think I started loving you when you tapped on my window," said Natee. "Do you remember the promise I made to you?"

"Yeah, that you would never tell my mom I took you to the potion shop, you even crossed your fingers," said Wesley.

"I promised you that I would stay your friend," said Natee. Natee held up her hand and crossed her fingers.

Wesley grabbed her hand. "I remember I said you didn't need to do that."

Natee took back her hand and held it up again with her fingers crossed. "Cross my fingers and not to spell. I will love you Wesley Candlewick for all eternity."

Wesley cried, "You didn't need to do that, Natee. You didn't need to do that."

Everyone wanted to know what was in the burlap bag. Natee showed up at the Poison Apple Tavern a day after she left the medical ward. She sat up on the bar and began to tell her story.

"It all started when I was thirteen. While I was in the Realm of Forbidden Magic I went through the rooms trying to remember as much information I could, because I thought I would never be there again," said Natee. She took a gulp of ale and continued.

"I was under the impression that Euphoria wanted to know where the portal to the Outside of the Universe was to end her life. That just wasn't true. She was going there to retrieve the..." Natee stopped held her breath and took another gulp of ale just for suspense. "...Hourglass of the Time Bandits."

Murmurs were heard through the tavern. Natee started talking again. "After Euphoria was trapped in the Realm of Forbidden Magic she wanted Mukul to retrieve the Hourglass for her to help her get out. He knew he couldn't do this alone. Euphoria was furious when Mukul sent me to retrieve his amulet and the whereabouts of the portal. As long as I didn't reveal where it was located it wouldn't move."

Harriet asked, "You did show Winston and the other wizards here where it was."

"Not really, Harriet. I took them there. I didn't show them the location that was on the paper," said Natee.

Someone asked, "So how did you get it?"

"I'm glad you asked that question. After I reincarnated Mukul..."

The whole tavern took in a breath of sudden fear.

"Ooooooowwwwwwwwuuuuu!"

"I thought James Candlewick must have told the whole magical world what I had done."

"James Candlewick knew?" was the question going around the crowd.

"It doesn't matter now, after I reincarnated Mukul he told me of Euphoria' plan. I convinced him that we should go after it anyways. I went to the Realm of Forbidden Magic and claimed my power over the realm just as Euphoria had done. I gathered up more information on the Outside of the Universe."

Someone back in the crowd yelled out, "Only a Black Witch could enter the Realm of Forbidden Magic. You have too much white magic."

Natee stood up on the bar. "Who said that? I dare you to show your face and say that directly to me."

No one came forward. So Natee pointed at the one that said it. "You're willing to say it hidden in a crowd, but not to my face, Elphaba? I know all your secrets. Do you still have that love spell on my Brother and how often do you use one on yourself?"

Elphaba just turned and left the tavern without a word.

Natee sat back down on the bar. "Mukul and I opened the portal and climbed down in using the silk rope of the spider that protected the entrance. There were miles of tunnels and small passages each filled with discarded debris. We would dig through it for days on end. It wasn't easy work and there were the throgs to contend with. They were little creatures that would bite and eat at your clothing and skin."

Wesley sat there with intense interest munching down finger niblets and slurping rich foamy carbonated witch hazelnut soda. Natee took another gulp of her mug of ale.

Natee looked directly at Wesley and smiled. "Each time I would show up I needed to recuperate before going back to the realm for more information to continue into the Outside of the Universe. One time a Grendel turned on me when I didn't have my full strength. It was an ugly fight between my magic and his sharp teeth and claws. After that when I went back I would kill just one to show them I was in charge." Natee's eyes shown that black haze in the whites of her eyes when she said that.

"This time when we went back to the Outside of the Universe, I had the location of the Hourglass. It was at the end of a narrow ledge. We held onto the rock face and slid our feet along the ledge. At the end was a small landing, just enough for one. Mukul thought he could get on it, but he was too large. He slipped and fell off the landing. He managed to grab the edge and held on."

Natee stopped and looked at the last of her ale in her mug. Tears began to show in her eyes. She sniffed back her tears and drank the remaining ale.

"I made it to the landing and held out my hands to pull Mukul up. He said…"

Natee stopped and wiped her nose to keep from crying. "…he said." Again she stopped. "Give me another mug of ale." She drank almost half of it down and burped.

"BBBBbbbuuuurrrrrppppp#$%! Excuse me."

"…he said, 'Go and have a long life with Wesley. He deserves to be loved by you more than I do'. And, and …, he let go of the edge." Natee drank the rest of her second ale down hard.

Wesley started to get up from his chair. Natee motioned him to sit back down.

"I'm not through yet. I stood there screaming his name but it was no use. I grabbed the Hourglass and slid my way back on the ledge. The throgs were waiting for me in clumps. They bit and snagged on my clothes. I swatted them off and more would jump at me. I got back to the spider silk rope and managed to climb out despite those nasty little creatures. The spider was waiting with a web made across my exit. I then did something that I learned from Peter Candlewick, how to wage war on spiders. I cut the sticky silk webbing off me and showed up on Wesley's door with the Hourglass of the Time Bandits."

She opened the bag and pulled it out for all to see.

"What are you going to do with the Hourglass?" asked a wizard.

"I don't know. Mukul and I worked so hard to find it that when it came to just leaving I decided to honor Mukul by bringing it back," said Natee.

"What does it do?" asked another wizard.

"That is for me to find out," said Natee.

When Wesley and Natee were alone sitting on his porch looking out at the stars he asked, "What is on the Outside of the Universe?"

Natee said, "Only Mukul."

"What did he mean that I deserve to be loved by you more than him?" asked Wesley.

"I don't know. Maybe that was his way of saying goodbye," said Natee.

"No! You do know. That was why you crossed your fingers and made that promise. He said something more before he let go, didn't he," said Wesley.

"No he didn't say anything else. It was all said way before hand. He told me everything, what the truth was and what had been lies. I told him I didn't care anymore. I loved him no matter what he had done in the past. He said that I should come to you and promise that I will always love you and to keep that promise because he didn't keep his to Euphoria," said Natee.

"Do you really love me?" asked Wesley.

Natee turned to Wesley and stared him right in the eyes, "Oh Wesley, yes, yes I really do. I have asked myself, when did I start to love you? And the answer kept coming back to when you tapped on my window the first time," said Natee. "I didn't need that drop of liquid sunset to kiss you. I used it as an excuse. And when we were cutting my birthday cake I pretended it was our wedding day."

"There is a party at the Poison Apple Tavern tomorrow night. Would you go with me as my girlfriend?" asked Wesley.

"Yes I will go with you as your girlfriend," said Natee.

The party was already going when Wesley and Natee had gotten to the Poison Apple Tavern. They mingled around talking to people, ate some appetizers.

Wesley and Natee made it over to the bar where he picked her up sat her on a bar stool. He got down on one knee and said "Natee Keystone, will you marry me?"

Natee looked at Wesley with a stunned expression. She knew that sometime soon he might ask. The whole crowd said in unison, "Well answer him?"

"Oh, I get it. This is my engagement party. You set me up Wesley. You know just for that I should say no, but everyone knows my answer, everyone has always known my answer. Isn't that right Sisters of the Q. Yes Wesley I will marry you and love you for all eternity," said Natee.

Then the party really got going. Natee's parents Howard and Melissa Keystone with Peter and Katee Candlewick came out of hiding to congratulate them.

Natee looked around for her Brothers and their wives. "Where are Fitzpatrick and Donavan?"

"They sent their regards that they couldn't make it. Something about not able to get a babysitter," said Wesley.

Natee magically turned the Hourglass of the Time Bandits over. Natee was gone for less than a moment, like time never even past.

Natee didn't take any time in convincing Gwendolyn and Elphaba to come to the party.

"You two, this is the last straw. I'm a sorceress am I, a black witch you say. I'm here to show you that my magic is so dark that they don't have a name for a witch like me. You are going to learn your place in this family and show me the respect I deserve."

Natee snapped her fingers and the three of them went to a special place of stone walls, ceiling, and floor. There were no windows and no doors. The room was lit up by brass flaming lamps that hung on the wall. She pointed her fingers at the two witches and slammed them into two chairs. The chairs grabbed them by their arms and ankles. The things that Natee showed them and did to them were horrific.

She held out poisonous snakes with long sharp fangs and forced the snakes to bite into the witches necks. Rats gnawed on their toes making them bloody stumps. Spider crawled all around them and sank their fangs into their skin sucking out blood.

Natee called on imaginary dungeon masters to hang them on the wall and whip them till they bled from their wounds across their backs. She called up flames to surround them. "I'm just beginning," Natee said laughing. The two un-mannered witches were dunked into hot boiling oil and then into freezing vats of sulfuric acid.

Natee wasn't bothered by any of what she was doing. "This is what you think of me. You made this room yourselves. I had nothing to do with what is going on."

The place changed. Now Gwendolyn, Elphaba, and Natee were nicely dressed in flowery southern bell clothing drinking tea and eating cake.

"This is how we should be acting toward each other. This is my place where I entertain bad mannered people. Sometimes they get called back from here to the last place. So I'll leave it up to you. Shall I just leave and let you two have your place of fun all to yourselves, hem? Or should we go to a party at the Poison Apple Tavern?"

Both Gwendolyn and Elphaba said, "No, no, no take us back with you."

"Then I'll see you at my party," said Natee.

A few minutes later her two Brothers and their wives walked in the double door of the Poison Apple Tavern. Fitzpatrick and Donavan came over to hug and congratulated Wesley and Natee. Their wives were the most pleasant that anybody had ever seen them, especially Melissa.

Wesley stared at Natee for split second. It seemed that she wasn't surprised that they showed up. Again her eyes showed a tinge of shading in white area. Wesley had picked up on this strange occurrence when other strange occurrences had happen.

Wesley wanted to ask, "Did you do something?" but didn't.

Chapter Twenty Six
How many for Breakfast?

The sand of time in the Hourglass was collected before time started. It is time that is unaccounted for. The one that possesses the Hourglass in essence could do anything and not be anywhere around to be blamed. So far that is all Natee knows about the Hourglass

Natee had collected magical powers, forbidden magical knowledge, a never empty bag of money, and the Hourglass of the Time Bandits. By the end of the month Natee Keystone will be Natee Candlewick

Something she hadn't expected now haunted her. It was quiet in her bedroom at the ranch house, too quiet. While she lay there on her bed she felt the terrible sensation of falling in darkness and never reaching the bottom.

"It's the blood stained rock. It is forever falling. I too am on the Outside of the Universe."

Natee knew the only person that would have the answer of what to do was Agnes. Of all the knowledge she collected from the room of forbidden and forgotten magical knowledge this problem was never encountered.

The next morning after a sleepless night of endless falling through darkness, Natee went to the Hidden Quiddity Potion Shop to see Agnes.

"Let's have some tea and you tell me how this rock with your blood on it got on the Outside of the Universe," said Agnes.

Natee told Agnes how she collected Mukul's ashes, "And in his pile was this rock that I thought had Mukul's blood on it. I left it in his ashes when I did the spell to reincarnate him. I didn't know it was my blood. There must be hundreds of rocks with my blood in the area between the reflection pond and the portal you and Harriet carried me out of."

"The difference is this blood stained rock was with Mukul's ashes during your reincarnation spell. In a sense you reincarnated a piece of you."

"But Mukul is dead. Shouldn't that blood stained rock be dead also?" asked Natee.

"Now there is an area of magic no one has gone into," said Agnes. "Mary might be the one that could find the answer. Maybe it is time for the Sister's of the Q to meet in a witch's coven."

It was that evening that the Sister's of the Q met at the home of Mary Pride. They sat in a circle with the chairs touching each other to close the circle.

Mary started by saying, "I found in this old book something that might shed some light on the situation. A witch was trying to make a double, or a twin, of herself. It was a different spell, but could explain what is going on. The rock had your dried dead blood on it. You reincarnated Mukul and the dead blood. With the witch she used her blood to make her double."

"A double didn't appear with Mukul though," said Natee.

"That is one of the differences. The witch that made the double found that she had also made a second soul. You may have reincarnated a piece of your soul," said Mary.

"But wouldn't that part of her soul perish the same way as Mukul?" asked April.

"Mukul died because he fell into the void of Outside of the Universe where there is no air to breathe. You are not dead, and you are connected to that piece of blood keeping it alive. That is still the mystery that must be resolved.

Agnes added another piece to the puzzle. "What do you supposed happened to Euphoria' amulet?"

The other witches together took in a deep breath as acknowledgment to a very good question.

Natee sat there nervous not saying a word. "They don't know I have Euphoria's green amulet."

The Sisters of the Q sat there and discussed possible solutions. None seemed plausible.

Then May Münter suggested, "If it is a piece of you then you could make it transmutate from the Outside of the Universe to here. Be careful that you do not transport to there."

Natee tried to meditate on the blood stained rock and bring it to her, "Maybe I'm trying too hard. Or the rock can't be moved from Outside to the Inside of the Universe."

The witch's circle ended without a final solution. Natee thank everyone for their help. She just didn't want to go home and be alone. She knew one place that might bring her some solitude and comfort. It was Mukul's shack up on the mountain.

In her bedroom Natee got out Mukul's staff and held it out in front of her. "I command you to take me to Mukul's shack."

Nothing happened. Natee was still in her bedroom. Natee was a little angry at this. She tried again. "I command you to transport me to my shack."

This time shimmering blue sparks shot out of the staff and Natee was whisked by the staff as a ball being shot out of a cannon. She tumbled around like she was in a clothes dryer. Natee slid down a ramp and into a hole falling endlessly.

"I'm on the Outside of the Universe," thought Natee.

Then with a muffled thud, Natee hit Mukul's old bed in his shack. She sat there for a moment waiting for everything to stop spinning. It was almost vomit time, but Natee kept still as she regained her equilibrium.

She laid down on the bed and stared at the wood roof ceiling. After a few minutes Natee sat up. "I don't feel that terrible sensation of falling in darkness and never reaching the bottom."

Next to her on the bed was the staff with the globe on top held there by carved dragon talon. Inside the globe was something that wasn't there before. Natee looked closely at the globe.

"It's the blood stained rock. The staff had to go and get the rock to bring me here, all of me."

Then she saw it move. Out of the rock came the ghostly face of Mukul swirling within the globe. He looked at Natee and smiled. From the globe he came out as a fiery storm and materialized in his full mortal state alive and well and said only two words.

"Immortality achieved."

He, the blood stained rock, and her were now all one. "Death no longer holds any bonds to the two of us," said Mukul.

"Time is on our side," said Mukul to Natee as he held up the staff and danced.

"Wait, you said three souls are needed for the magical math. Who's makes up the third soul?" said Natee with a questionable look.

"Yes indeed I did say that. Your soul is leading, Wesley is following. That leaves me all alone to myself, hee hee," laughed Mukul with a glaring stare and smirk.

"Wesley's, you had me make that unbreakable promise to love him for all eternity to complete the spell didn't you?" asked Natee.

Mukul didn't answer, he just smiled and went back to dancing. Natee's soul was inflamed with the treachery of Mukul's trickery.

"I'll get even with him if it takes all my magic to do it!" Natee promised herself.

Mukul said his goodbyes around town and finally disappeared to places unknown.

Natee spent some time at Mukul's shack changing it for her and Wesley to live there. She hired a magical construction firm of Trolls and Ogres that built an elegant two story house decorated with gold fixtures, plush hand woven carpets, and finely polished wood furniture in the place of the old shack.

"This is my home for now on," said Natee.

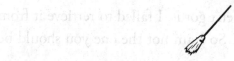

Mukul stopped in at the Black Forest pub during his travels. The nymph fairy named Esmeralda who owned the Black Forest pub was tending bar when Mukul came in.

"I haven't seen you, oh at least six years Mukul," said Esmeralda.

"I've been busy Esmeralda. Listen I need a little credit, I'm almost ready to make the deal of the century," said Mukul.

Six men quietly came into the Black Forest pub. They took a booth where they could clearly see Mukul. Mukul peered over at the six men knowing why they were there.

Esmeralda left Mukul at the bar and tended to the newcomers herself. "Hello, I'm Esmeralda. This is my place so no rough stuff okay? What will you have to drink?"

"I'll have the thyme on my hands sandwich with a pitcher of dark ale," said the first man.

The other five men nodded in agreement.

"Okay six thyme on my hands sandwiches with pitchers of dark ale to drink. Anything else?" asked Esmeralda.

"Yeah, have that wizard come join us," said the first man.

Esmeralda moved through the bar opening and handed in the food order to the cook. She got back to Mukul.

"You are wanted at their table. Like I told them no rough stuff," said Esmeralda.

Mukul walked over to the table. While in route Mukul grabbed an empty chair from another table. He slid it up to the table of the six men and sat down.

"So here's the deal. I haven't got it. I failed to retrieve it from the Outside of the Universe. So I am not the one you should be talking to," said Mukul.

"Here are your, six thyme on my hands sandwiches with six dark ales," said Esmeralda.

"And the way I see it, finders keepers losers weepers. If I understand the situation correctly, you lost the Hourglass of Time right after you stole the sand and sealed it inside," announced Mukul.

"Who should we be talking to about our hourglass?"

"I don't give out valuable information," said Mukul.

"How much?"

"One million wizens in the Wizard's Swiss Bank," whispered Mukul.

The man tapped on a stone tablet with a stick. "Done, minus what we have already paid you already, now who?"

"Natee Keystone of Broomstick," said Mukul as he stood up and left the Black Forest Pub to a new destination.

"A wedding, a wedding, there's going to be a wedding," sang Harriet.

"Don't get too excited. We may not be the caterers. I'm sure Natee remembers her thirteenth birthday cake with the black candles adorning it," said Agnes.

Natee came into the potion shop just about the time when Agnes and Harriet were talking about that subject with a favor to ask, "Will you cater my wedding? I want it just like my thirteenth birthday, black candles and all."

"At the cemetery?" asked Harriet.

"Yes is that okay?" queried Natee.

"And how many black candles do you want on the cake this time?" asked Harriet.

"Thirteen would still be good," said Natee.

"Yes of course it is. We will handle all the details," said Agnes.

"Hand fasting would be more appropriate than marriage vows," said Harriet.

"I never said anything about this. I used the Hourglass of Time to fix one little detail in my past that bothered me."

Natee had a very sheepish expression on her face.

"Actually Wesley and I have been hand fasted since my thirteenth birthday party. Zweig the Wizard preformed the ceremony just before we cut the cake." explained Natee.

"Zweig was here when you were thirteen?" questioned Harriet.

"Was he someone important?"

"Ah, no not really, just a name in passing," answered Harriet.

Harriet whispered to Agnes, "Did you hear that? Zweig the Wizard was here when she was thirteen years old."

There is a castle in the Border Forest of England that overlooks a large valley. The town within that valley is called Dragonstep. It had been said, if one would fly on a broom stick and looked at the valley, it looked as if a dragon had stepped down making a talon print in the earth.

That castle was where the sorceress Vigoda Whetstone had lived. It was the same castle those centuries later Wanda Whetstone had gone to hide after she caused the dragon pox outbreak in

Broomstick. Now after years of being a source of black tales, Wanda had opened it up to visitors as a place to vacation at. It was a perfect spot for a honeymoon.

Natee selected the sleeping chamber that overlooked the courtyard with a large bay window. Old world drapery hung on each side of the window. There was a canopy bed, dressing table, and two matching nightstands that decorated the room.

The sky was crystal clear at the beginning of the night. The stars glistened within the heavens. That was to change in the middle of the night. As Natee slept, her magic was at work once again giving her another in a series of her nightmares that had started just before she turned thirteen.

Outside the castle the clouds were forming. A tremendous storm was lurking on the horizon. Then it started. First there was a flash of lightning followed by the thunder clap.

The wind picked up and whistled it eerie tune through the halls of the castle. The raindrops started to hit the large bay window with a steady beat. The symphony was about to begin.

Wesley watched both the storm outside and Natee sleeping. Her movements were in sync with the bolts of Lightning. When she would twist or jerk, a streak of hot electricity would zip across the sky. Her hands clenched and tugged on the bedding when the loud clap and crash of thunder that shook the bay window. This went on for most of the night. There were small cringes and small lightning to sudden convulsions with powerful grandeur of nature's force.

Natee settled down and the storm dissipated. Both she and nature were sleeping peacefully as dawn hinted to its arrival soon.

A couple hours later Wesley quietly got out of bed and pulled the drapes from each side of the window closed and went down the stairway from the upper levels of the castle. The banisters were polished showing their beautiful centuries old wood grains. At midlevel before the stair split going two ways was a stained glass window depicting a great dragon with wings outstretched stepping down with one talon in a valley.

At the bottom of the stairs was a foyer where Wesley took a side passage to a door that led into the main hall. Breakfast was already being served to one other guest. He too was staying at the castle for his honeymoon.

The young newly wedded wizard asked Wesley, "How about that storm last night?"

Wesley sat down to the breakfast plate that was served him. "Natee, my uh wife, she tossed and turned with the storm."

"My bride slept quietly all through that storm. She could sleep through anything," said the newly wedded wizard.

"That storm last night, I confess was conjured up by Natee. She was in total control of it. The way she moved in her sleep was like she was throwing the lightning bolts herself," said Wesley. "All these years I didn't understand her psychotic way of doing magic, until last night."

Wesley leaned over to his breakfast companion and began to whisper, "My wife could be a sorceress…"

Wesley's conversation was interrupted when at the far end of the hall, two extremely huge double doors with carved panels and marble inlaid patterns were swung open.

Natee was standing there in a long purple velvet dress with bellowing sleeves and a high collar. Behind her was the stained glass window that depicted a great dragon with wings outstretched stepping down with one talon in a valley.

The sun was shining through the stained glass window lighting up the scene with vibrant colors all around Natee. She was staring directly at Wesley with sharp eyes.

Wesley could feel that Natee had changed somehow last night. "…a saucer of butter needed for the toast," Wesley finished saying.

The other wizard looked strangely at Wesley for what he had just said, and then he turned his head to the direction that Wesley was staring.

Natee came over to Wesley and put her arms around him from behind. "You're not telling family secrets outside the sleeping chambers are you?" asked Natee.

Wesley answered, "We were just discussing last night's weather. You slept right through the violent storm that came through here."

Natee sat down to her breakfast plate. "You're right about a sorceress, oh I meant to say 'a saucer' of butter is needed," said Natee with a small laugh.

Wesley felt a little uncomfortable for the duration of breakfast. Later while taking a walk he said, "I know it was you that caused and controlled that storm last night. What were you dreaming about?"

"It was about a struggle with death over the possession of the Hourglass of the Time Bandits. I had won the complete ownership of the Hourglass. Can one have too much magical power?" asked Natee.

"I'm worried for you Natee. Are you controlling your powers or are they controlling you? Don't go down the path of black magic, Natee. Death waits for those involved with destructive consequences," said Wesley.

Natee looked at Wesley with secrets behind her eyes. "I'm

not worried about death. He has no contract on me, you, or Mukul. And I am in full control of all my magical power, from the whitest amulet from Shasta to my personal black amulet. Together Wesley, we are the most powerful Candlewick family members ever."

"Don't say that too loud. James Candlewick might hear you," said Wesley. "He knows everything that goes on in this family."

"Not anymore. James told me himself he can't see me, I'm invisible to him," said Natee with sheer determination in her eyes.

"Kiss me Wesley."

While they kissed, Wesley's love intensified for her. He felt a surge of magical power within him and knew she was right about everything she had said. Natee darkened Wesley's glass window to his soul, but brighten it with her love.

The Keystones settled into their new lifestyle of private ownership of small businesses. The strip mall had once again a greeting card shop, and a florist. Melissa's Wine and Cheese was right next to Keystone's Bakery.

No one really knew what Natee and Wesley were doing or where they were. Natee was still testing what they can do with the Hourglass of the Time Bandits.

"Let's try..." Natee turned the hourglass over. Wesley watched Natee and the hourglass disappear.

Suddenly Natee was back with her two hands gripping the hourglass holding on to dear life, "Nope, nope, nope, not that spell."

One time Natee came back to Broomstick and found everything was completely different. "Olsen's Bakery, the gift card and florist, Wesley's Wine and Cheese?"

Natee went into Wesley's Wine and Cheese. At the cash register was Wesley.

"Can I interest you in a five wine and cheese taste?" said Wesley to Natee.

"Wesley, it's me, Natee."

"Am I supposed to know you?" asked Wesley.

"Yes, I'm your wife. We live up on Shadow Creek Mountain. We have known each other since we were thirteen," declared Natee waving her one empty hand while the other hand held the hourglass.

"Who put you up to this? Was it Dunkin? If it was you would know how much Dunkin is a practical joker," said Wesley with a smile and a little laugh.

"I erased my life. No you can't do that," said Natee while waving the hourglass back and forth trying to slow down the sand.

Then Natee turned the hourglass over hoping it would reverse whatever she did in time. "Go back to my mistake."

Natee appeared in her house with Wesley still standing there watching Natee as she held the hourglass still as the last of the sand fell to the bottom.

"I think I have had enough for now. However, I do know where I need to be."

The Time Bandits knew exactly where to go in Broomstick to find Miss Natee Keystone. It was down an alley to the crumbling in decay part of Broomstick known as the Troll District.

Down in the Root Cellar the Time Bandits sat in a corner booth away from the other magical creatures.

"Our special is Cheeseburgers, French fries, and two pitchers of beer with six mugs," said Natee playing a nymph waitress.

Natee playing a nymph waitress showed up with the two pitchers of beer and six iced beer mugs. She poured the one man's beer from a pitcher.

"Got a name big guy?"

"Thyme."

"Well Mr. Thyme, I get off work at closing time."

After Natee playing a nymph waitress brought the cheeseburgers and fries, Mr. Goose the Troll dragged over a chair.

"Time Bandits, what can I do for you?" asked Mr. Goose.

"Where is this girl Natee Keystone?"

"I can do better, How about the whereabouts of two knotems related to the witch you are after," said Mr. Goose.

Trolls like Mr. Goose deal in gold, true gold, solid brick gold.

Two solid bars of gold were placed on the table in front of Mr. Goose.

"Next to the cemetery is a bakery, ask for Howard Keystone. Melissa Keystone is in the next one over. It's a wine and cheese store."

As the Time Bandits were leaving the Root Cellar a real nymph waitress was also leaving. "Hey big guy, want to see my house in the woods?"

"Right now I have too much time on my hands and it's wasting away in Margarita Ville. I'll catch you next time I'm in town."

It was a sunny day with a good assortment of people coming into the Keystone's Bakery. Howard was happy to have the extra help.

"I want to see what makes you love baking," said Natee hugging her dad.

It was right after the lunch rush the Time Bandits came into the bakery. Howard was just finishing up with a couple buying a cinnamon apple pie for a picnic in the town's cemetery.

"Can I help find something sweet?" asked Howard.

"Where is your daughter?"

"I'm right here," said Natee as she turned around dressed in a white baker's uniform.

"I knew you were coming. I even brought the Hourglass of Time," said Natee.

Natee sat the hourglass on the counter. One of the Time Bandits went to pick up the hourglass.

"Before you take it, do you know what the hourglass does?"

"We'll use it to fix the mistakes in the timeline," said the first Time Bandit.

"What mistakes, no don't tell me I already know some."

Natee paused then said, "If the hourglass belongs to you then turn it over and the hourglass will go with you. If it doesn't belong to you, you will disappear and you will never be heard from again," explained Natee.

The six men all touched the Hourglass of Time while one of them turned it over. The sand in the top started falling down through the pinched glass orifice. One by one the six men disappeared, the last one leaving the Hourglass of Time on the counter with all the sand sitting at the bottom.

"Did you know that was going to happen?" asked Natee's dad Howard.

"I was guessing," said Natee.

"Where did you send them?" asked Howard.

"I didn't send them anywhere. They selected from two choices," said Natee.

"There are only two choices in time?" queried Howard.

Natee said as she picked up the Hourglass of Time off the counter, "There are two sides to time. Time spent not doing what you want to do and time spent doing what you want to do. I found out it all depends on how one turns over the Hourglass of Time."

Natee winked as she turned over the Hourglass. "See you next time Dad. It's time for this witch to go home," said Natee as she disappeared.

Printed in the United States
By Bookmasters